PENGUIN CLASSICS

LOVE STANDS ALONE

M.L. THANGAPPA taught Tamil for over twenty-five years in the various colleges of the Puducherry government until his retirement in 1994. He has published a number of books of poetry and essays in Tamil and has translated from Tamil into English Sangam poetry, and the songs of Ramalinga Swamigal, Subramania Bharati and Bharathidasan. He was awarded the Bharathidasan Award (1991) and the Sirpi Literary Award (2007) for lifetime achievement in poetry. He has won the Sahitya Akademi awards for both children's literature and translation. His translation of *Muttollayiram* has appeared in Penguin Classics as *Red Lilies and Frightened Birds* (edited by A.R. Venkatachalapathy).

A.R. VENKATACHALAPATHY has taught history at Manonmaniam Sundaranar University, Tirunelveli, the University of Madras and the University of Chicago. Currently he is professor at the Madras Institute of Development Studies, Chennai. He has published widely on the social, cultural and intellectual history of colonial Tamil Nadu, both in Tamil and in English.

PRAISE FOR THE BOOK

'For those who cannot read them in the original, poems can only be as good as their translators. In this respect, the poets of the Tamil anthologies have been very fortunate, perhaps more so than any other group of Indian poets, past or present. Beginning with A.K. Ramanujan, they've had a chain of exceptional translators, in which M.L. Thangappa is the most recent, and in some ways the most surprising, link. The surprise lies in the fact that Thangappa is a Puducherry-based Tamil teacher, whereas I had always thought that the best translations of Indian poetry would be made by scholars working in the Western academy.

'The 160-odd poems in *Love Stands Alone* are often quite short, though there's enough going on in them to fill a chapter in a fat novel. Keeping the voice low, the tone level, they say the most heartbreaking, or urgent, or joyful things. This is why we're still listening to them, our ears pricked, after 2000 years. Luckily for us, Thangappa translates several of the longer poems too. Reading them is like watching one of those folk performances in which women dance while balancing pots on their heads. You watch with your heart in your mouth, for one false step can bring the whole thing crashing down. But Thangappa carries it off again and again. More than once I caught myself whistling'—Arvind Krishna Mehrotra

'M.L. Thangappa's translations from the Sangam anthologies possess a rare precision and accuracy, crafted in a voice that is vivid, supple, and uniquely his own. Classical Tamil and modern English are separated by what can seem like unbridgeable distances of time, form, idiom and culture. Yet, reading Thangappa, I am surprised—even astonished—to find the thought of south Indian poets of two millennia ago newly, and seemingly effortlessly, embodied'—Whitney Cox, School of Oriental and African Studies

'Thangappa's translations are marked by a serenity and an assurance that owe to utter familiarity with the source text. He grasps the modernity inherent in the source texts almost by habit and conveys this understanding effortlessly in his translations'—*Indian Express*

'Among the qualities of this corpus of poetry are its diversity of situations and its vivid relation of the natural world to human moods and predicaments'—*Mint*

'Life is impermanent, most art sinks without a trace, even the true names of these bards are lost, but something elemental endures in this literature. Only that which is timeless remains. What Thangappa, one of many torchbearers, passes down in *Love Stands Alone* is a triumph'—*New Indian Express*

'Penguin has been bringing out gems from rich Indian literature and this latest volume from the Sangam poetry definitely is a jewel'—*Organiser*

LOVE STANDS ALONE

Selections from Tamil Sangam Poetry

Translated by

M.L. THANGAPPA

Edited and introduced by

A.R. VENKATACHALAPATHY

PENGUIN BOOKS

PENGUIN BOOKS
Published by the Penguin Group
Penguin Books India Pvt. Ltd, 11 Community Centre, Panchsheel Park,
New Delhi 110 017, India
Penguin Group (USA) Inc., 375 Hudson Street, New York, New York 10014,
USA
Penguin Group (Canada), 90 Eglinton Avenue East, Suite 700, Toronto,
Ontario, M4P 2Y3, Canada (a division of Pearson Penguin Canada Inc.)
Penguin Books Ltd, 80 Strand, London WC2R 0RL, England
Penguin Ireland, 25 St Stephen's Green, Dublin 2, Ireland
(a division of Penguin Books Ltd)
Penguin Group (Australia), 707 Collins Street, Melbourne,
Victoria 3008, Australia (a division of Pearson Australia Group Pty Ltd)
Penguin Group (NZ), 67 Apollo Drive, Rosedale, Auckland 0632,
New Zealand (a division of Pearson New Zealand Ltd)
Penguin Group (South Africa) (Pty) Ltd, Block D, Rosebank Office Park,
181 Jan Smuts Avenue, Parktown North, Johannesburg 2193, South Africa

Penguin Books Ltd, Registered Offices: 80 Strand, London WC2R 0RL,
England

First published in Viking by Penguin Books India 2010
Published in Penguin Books 2013

Translation copyright © M.L. Thangappa 2010
Introduction copyright © A.R. Venkatachalapathy 2010

All rights reserved

10 9 8 7 6 5 4 3 2 1

ISBN 9780143103974

Typeset in Joanna MT by Eleven Arts, New Delhi
Printed at Sanat Printers, Kundli, Haryana

for Tha. Kovendhan (1932–2004)
in memoriam

[T]he epithet 'ancient wisdom' was used for them . . . many of them were elegant versifiers, amiable companions, consummate courtiers, and venerated wise men all in one. It was this many-sided personality of the bards, which . . . gave them a distinct identity and scope of expression that has secured their position in history. In later ages the poems of these bards soon came to be considered unique. The exclusive expression *canror ceyyul,* 'poetry of the noble ones' was especially used for their works. When referring to the poetry of this age, the medieval commentators respectfully employ this appellation.

—K. Kailasapathy, *Tamil Heroic Poetry*

In the desolate, rain-forsaken land
the twisted *kalli*'s pods
open with a crackle
frightening the mating pigeons
with their close-knit downy feathers.

He has left me languishing.
'In search of wealth,' he said.
He did not mind the risks on the way.

If it comes to that,
then in this world
wealth has all support
and love must stand alone.

KURUNTHOKAI 174

Contents

Introduction
Tradition, Talent, Translation
A.R. Venkatachalapathy

'Poetry cannot swerve from tradition,' declares Tholkappiyam, the defining grammatical treatise on Sangam literature. Such unequivocality about the place of tradition must seem to be at odds with, say, English poetry where, as T.S. Eliot famously observed, tradition is only occasionally invoked and usually to deplore its absence. Contrary to the censorial and approbative sense in which it is often used in English, tradition permeates, defines and approves much of Tamil poetry, most especially classical Tamil poetry. The Tamil language's claim to classical status rests on the corpus of literature commonly known as Sangam literature. The over 2,000 poems which make up this corpus are breathtaking in their directness, subtle in their nuances and have an astonishing contemporary quality.

According to tradition there were three Sangams, or academies, in ancient Tamil Nadu where poets congregated to debate and authorize literary works. The first Sangam is said to have flourished south of present-day Kanyakumari, now submerged, in the ancient Pandyan city of Then-Madurai. Consisting of as many as 4,449 poets, it is said to have reigned for 4,440 years. The second Sangam, in Kapadapuram, is said to have flourished for 3,700 years with 3,700 poets. Both these Sangams, each consisting of fifty-nine core poets, are believed to have been engulfed by the sea and the works lost. The third or last Sangam, in historical Madurai, continued for 1,850 years with forty-nine core poets and another 449 contributing poets. All the surviving works are said to be from this Sangam, except Tholkappiyam said to be from the second Sangam. As the fantastic numbers would indicate there is undoubtedly more myth than fact even though one cannot discount the validity of historical memory about some massive tsunami that could have engulfed an earlier culture. As even K. Kailasapathy, a scholar not known for his sympathy towards Tamil identity politics concedes, 'it seems likely that persistent traditions about lost books might embody genuine memories'.[1] Understandably, this myth has had a powerful hold on the Tamil cultural mind and has lived on for about a millennium and a half and has been phenomenally productive in terms of the many literary and artistic representations it has spawned.

The word 'Sangam' itself, however, does not occur in the sense of an academy in the corpus of literature known as Sangam literature, which is a useful and convenient shorthand for identification. The first occurrence of the Sangam as a Tamil academy dates from the Bhakti movement of the seventh to ninth centuries CE. This popular movement which had a far-reaching impact on the religious map of the Indian subcontinent, and gave the concept of bhakti to the religious vocabulary of the subcontinent, began its career in the Tamil country with a strident anti-Buddhist/Jain content. The medieval bhakti poets Andal and Thirugnanasambandar's references to Sanga-Tamil (Tamil of the Sangam[s]) are undoubtedly inspired by the Buddhist and Jain Sangams established in the fifth century in the Tamil country. By the ninth century, with the convergence of language (Tamil) and religion (Saivism) the tradition of the Sangam was further embellished. The Pandyan kings, in their stylized *meikeerthis* or *prasastis*, engraved on numerous stone inscriptions, began to routinely claim that their ancestors built the city of Madurai and founded the Sangam there. In the tenth-century *Iraiyanar Agapporul Urai*, the myth is thoroughly fleshed out with the above fanciful numbers. Further, the supreme lord Siva and his son Murugan were counted among the poets of the Sangam. An elaborate mythology where Siva himself composed a poem—the celebrated *Kurunthokai* 40 which was challenged by the presiding poet Nakkeeran—was constructed. This story which is first alluded to in the medieval bhakti poet Thirunavukkarasar's poems gets elaborated in the various *Thiruvilaiyadal Puranam* versions starting from the eleventh century. The tradition of Sangam played a central role in the primacy achieved by Madurai in Tamil literary imagination and in the Saiva religious world.

The extant corpus is made of two sets of eighteen works. The *pathinen melkanakku* or the 'major/higher eighteen' consists of the *Ettuthokai* (The Eight Anthologies) and the *Pathupattu* (The Ten Long Poems). To this must be added the outstanding work of, among other things, linguistic analysis and scholarship, the grammar *Tholkappiyam*. *Thirukkural* has pride of place in the *pathinen keelkanakku* or the 'minor/lower eighteen'. It is now common to designate the first eighteen as Sangam literature proper; the other eighteen being now considered post-Sangam.

The eight anthologies consist of *Ainkurunuru, Kurunthokai, Nattrinai, Akananuru, Kalithokai, Pathittrupathu, Paripadal* and *Purananuru*. *Thirumurugattrupadai* (also called *Pulavar Attrupadai*), *Porunar Attrupadai, Sirupan Attrupadai, Perumpan Attrupadai, Mullai Pattu, Madurai Kanji, Nedunalvadai, Kurinji Pattu, Pattinappalai* and *Malaipadukadam* (also called *Kuthar Attrupadai*) make up the *Pathupattu*.

The poems in this corpus total 2,381 composed by as many as 473 poets. For reasons elaborated below there are a number of missing poems in the Sangam corpus: two poems (129 and 130) are missing from *Ainkurunuru*, one from *Nattrinai* (234), twenty from *Pathittrupathu* (1–10 and 91–100); more than half of *Paripadal* is missing. And in the iconic *Purananuru* itself not only are two poems missing but as many as forty-three poems are available only in mutilated form. Further some colophons and authors' names are also not available.

The dating of the Sangam works is highly vexatious. What is clear is that the date of composition and the date of anthologization are different and perhaps separated by as many as a few centuries. There is a huge scholarly industry, in Tamil Nadu and around the world, turning out monographs and articles on dating and chronology. Often the dating of this corpus is the litmus test for one's Tamil-ness—the older the date assigned the more authentic a Tamil one is. Such early dating is also a reaction to certain ideological strands which delight in pulling down the dates and drawing Sanskrit parallels for every Tamil achievement. Not surprisingly, therefore, it is often very difficult to clear the crabgrass of argument and polemic to arrive at a reasoned conclusion. But based on archaeological (especially the hoards of Roman coins found in many parts of Tamil Nadu), epigraphic, sociological and linguistic evidence, it is now certain that some of the poems may have been composed as early as in the second century BCE; the later limit being the first couple of centuries of the Common Era. The really clinching evidence comes from the recent consolidation of the early epigraphic record by Iravatham Mahadevan who has dated the Tamil Brahmi inscriptions with their striking correlation to Sangam names and terms to the third century BCE. However, scholarly attempts to establish relative chronology have been more successful.

It might be useful here to understand the structure of the anthologies. *Ainkurunuru*, consisting of 500 *akam* poems (see below) which vary in length between three and six lines, is divided into a hundred poems for each of the five *thinais* (see below), organized in tens. *Kurunthokai*, *Nattrinai* and *Akananuru* consist of 400 *akam* poems each. The organizing principle is the length of the poems. *Kurunthokai* consists of four to eight lines,[2] *Nattrinai*, nine to twelve and *Akananuru*, thirteen to thirty-one. *Akananuru* itself is divided into three books: *Kalittriyanainirai*, *Manimidaipavalam* and *Nithilakkovai* based on the arresting phrases occurring in them even though the logic of the division is not evident. Within the *Akananuru* all odd numbered poems belong to Palai *thinai*, thus accounting for half of the poems. Poems in the sequence of 2, 8, 12, 18 . . . belong to Kurinji; poems in the sequence of 4, 14, 24 . . . are Mullai; poems in the sequence of 6, 16, 26 . . . belong to Marutam and every tenth poem (10, 20, 30 . . .) is in Neidal *thinai*. It is evident that these three anthologies were put together at the same time. *Purananuru*, the prime text in *puram* (see below), was also probably anthologized at this time. *Pathittrupathu*, with ten decads, each one in praise of a Chera king containing a wealth of information which can be teased out for historical evidence, is also considered to belong to the early stratum of the Sangam corpus.

Kalithokai, in the *kali* metre, as distinct from the *akaval* metre (analogous to blank verse in English), the prosodic form par excellence of Sangam poetry, consists of 150 long poems. Similarly *Paripadal* is written in the *pari* metre. There is a scholarly consensus that these two works belong to a later period. Of the *Pathupattu*, *Thirumurugattrupadai* is considered to be a very late work—a fact buttressed by its inclusion in the Saiva literary canon. The poems in the *Pathupattu* range from 103–782 lines.

As for the poets themselves, as many as 473 have contributed to the corpus. Of these about 250 poets wrote only one poem each. Among the poets are thirty women with 154 compositions; the most outstanding being the hugely venerated Avvaiyar. Just over a 100 poems remain anonymous. Some of the most prolific and important poets are Kapilar (235 poems), Orampokiyar (110), Paranar (eighty-five), Perunkatunko (sixty-eight), Avvaiyar (fifty-nine) and Nakkeerar (thirty-seven). Some kings and queens count among the poets. It is evident that the poets were greatly venerated and respected. If within the poems themselves the poets are said to be repositories of ancient wisdom with prophetic abilities and whose praise the kings and patrons seek, the colophons always reserve the honorific plural (with the *ar* suffix) for the poets while the kings are referred to in the singular (with the *an* suffix).

Defining the Tradition

How does one make sense of this enormous, varied and rich corpus? An indispensable text for understanding much of Sangam poetry is the grammatical text *Tholkappiyam*. It is somewhat restrictive to call it only a grammar for it encompasses so much that it presents a veritable cosmology, a unified world view. In the depth and range of its linguistic analysis it can be compared only to Panini's *Ashtadhyayi* even though the Sanskrit grammar does not cover what is certainly a unique part of *Tholkappiyam*, its brilliant classification and analysis of 'content' or 'subject matter'. Consisting of 1,610 verses in the pithy *nurpa* (*sutra*) form, the text of *Tholkappiyam* is divided into three books: *Ezhuthu* (letters—mostly concerned with phonetics), *Chol* (words—largely concerned with morphology and syntax) and *Porul* (content or subject matter—poetics or rhetoric). Little is known about the author except that he is called Tholkappiyar after the work he composed and that he could be a Jain. Dating is once again a vexed question but like the earliest of Sangam poetry itself *Tholkappiyam* was composed a little before the Common Era. Interpolations in the text also cannot be ruled out—though it has become a game with some scholars to dismiss as an interpolation any *nurpa* that does not fit their scheme. Dating apart, that *Tholkappiyam* was drawing from a range of much earlier authorities is certain: there are innumerable references to 'they said', 'it is said', 'so say the learned ones' in the text that Tholkappiyar was coming in a long tradition of grammarians is beyond dispute. For some schools of thought in the Tamil world *Tholkappiyam* is tradition. Whether *Tholkappiyam*'s theorizing is based on the Sangam poems or the poems were composed in conformity with its prescriptions is however not certain. V.Sp. Manickam, in his magisterial study of the Tamil concept of love, asserts that the Sangam poems were written *after* the elaborate and minute codification of the grammar of love poetry. Many others have held the contrary, logical view that grammar follows literature. But few would gainsay the absolute indispensability of *Tholkappiyam* to understand the Sangam poems.

Tholkappiyam divides the content and subject matter of all literature into two complementary and overarching categories: *akam* and *puram*, concepts which are now slowly passing into English without italicization. These two terms are extraordinarily complex, defying any simple translation. The authoritative *Tamil Lexicon* defines *akam* as inside, interior, heart, mind, breast, sexual pleasure, house, agricultural tract, the theme of love, subject, etc. *Puram* is defined as the 'other' of *akam*: outside, exterior, heroism, bravery, side, back, gossip and backbiting, partiality, place, tax-free land, wild tract, etc. These binaries indicate the complementarity of these two concepts. That the *Lexicon* lists nearly 200 compound words with *puram* and scores with *akam* would indicate the wide semantic use these have been put to over the centuries.[3]

For *Tholkappiyam*, *akam* concerns the interior or love and conjugal life. The *akam* poems are concerned with love in all its varied situations: pre-marital and marital; clandestine and illicit; conjugal happiness and infidelity; separation and union. This amorous life is divided into five thinais: Kurinji, Mullai, Marutam, Neidal and Palai. *Thinais* are physiographical regions in which the love poems are set. *Tholkappiyam* classifies the recurrent themes in the following ascending hierarchy—into mudhal (the first theme), karu (the seed theme) and uri (the essential theme). *Mudhal* refers to time and place. (The hills for Kurinji thinai, the pastures and woods for Mullai; the countryside and plains for Marutam; the seaside for Neidal. While there is no desert proper in the Tamil country, Palai refers to the wilderness and dried-up Kurinji and Mullai land during hot summers.) Similarly the time of day and seasons appropriate for the above five thinais, respectively, are night and cool season; late evenings and monsoons; mornings and all seasons; nightfall and all seasons; midday and summer. *Karu* refers to the deity, food, flora, fauna, drum, occupation, music, etc. that are current in that particular physiographical region. The uri porul is the essence of akam poetry and it defines akam poetry:

Kurinji: clandestine meetings of lovers
Mullai: hopeful waiting of the wife
Marutam: the infidelity of the man and the sulks of his wife
Neidal: the wife's anxious wait for the husband's return
Palai: the lover's departure and travel through wilderness in search of wealth, education or adventure

While these five thinais occupy pride of place there are two more categories of 'inferior' love: Kaikkilai, one-sided or unrequited love, and Perumthinai, mismatched love or excessive lust. Whether these belong to akam proper is a subject of much debate which will not detain us here; as we shall see below, post-Tholkappiyam literary theoreticians include these under puram. Suffice it to say that only 4 and 10 poems come under these thinais, respectively, in the akam anthologies.

Whether the thinai classification amounts to only a literary convention or it represents actual social reality is once again the subject of much scholarly debate. K. Sivathamby, the Marxist scholar, has argued that the thinai divisions reflect the uneven development of productive forces in ancient Tamil society. Perhaps at this point it may be appropriate to digress into a brief description of Sangam society. Collating the extant historical evidence and scholarship it is more or less certain that ancient Tamil society was a relatively simple social formation moving towards an early agrarian state. As the historian

Kesavan Veluthat summarizes the scholarship, the principle of social organization was kinship and 'the economy and society [were] characterised by subsistence production, redistribution, reciprocity and patronage.'[4] 'One could perceive the residue of an undifferentiated social order in the poems,'[5] as K. Kailasapathy remarks, and evidently that society was in transition towards a more complex social formation with the emerging institution of the state. It has also been suggested by many scholars, in very moving terms, that the Sangam poets in many instances were singing the passing of an ancient, egalitarian system. An important aspect of ancient Tamil society is, notwithstanding social segmentation, the virtual absence of caste (as a *system*), or status based on ascription. Further there is certainly no presence of institutionalized religion. Buddhism, Jainism and Brahminism have only an incipient presence in the literature. Largely for these reasons, ancient Tamil society is seen as pre-Aryan—something that has provided intellectual ammunition to many modern-day emancipatory social and political movements.

Most strikingly, in addition, the literary models adopted show little or no sign of Sanskrit influence. On the contrary, George Hart has argued that 'northern traditions [were] drawing more and more from the folk traditions' of the South even though he defensively qualifies it by adding, in italics for added emphasis, that 'I do not suggest that there was any significant borrowing by northern sources directly from Tamil.' He contends that the Tamil literary elements entering the North were mediated through Maharashtrian Prakrit as evidenced by Hala's *Gatasaptasati* which 'is remarkably close to the earlier Tamil anthologies'.[6]

Recently, the *thinai* system has been seized by nativist and anti-Orientalist scholars as an alternative literary theory that challenges Eurocentric literary models. K. Ayyappa Panicker, the celebrated modern Malayalam poet, was in the vanguard of this theoretical movement. The emerging field of eco-criticism too has found the *thinai* model to be enriching.

In sum, then, the *akam* poetry deals with love and conjugal life in all its variety but set in specific contexts. It is interesting that the *thinais* are all named after flowers which probably indicate totemic origins.

The wild boar was strong
and sure-footed.
His mate had a rough
bristling coat
and flabby teats.
A hunter watched the boar
and crouched for him
in a cave by the path.
He killed the boar
with his arrows.
Later, in the village
the hunter's dark-haired wife
distributed pork
among her kinsfolk.
These are the mountains
from where you come.
You may not be afraid
of the night's treachery,
or of the jungle and the river bed,
where an angry tusker waits
to fight a tiger.

Only I am afraid
for your safety.
For along the narrow mountain path
there are many termite hills
and the bears come in crowds
to dig them up.

(what the girl said to the lover anxious for his safety)

Kurinji
—Kapilar

NATTRINAI 336

Here is a classic Kurinji poem by Kapilar renowned for his mastery of this particular thinai. The physical location is the richly forested hills and the time is night. References are made to the boar, the bear, the tiger, the elephant and termites, and the hunter and his family and kin. In this context is set the union of the lovers and the girl's fear of their nightly clandestine meetings. Thus each akam poem is situated in a specific context. The matching of the thematic content with the physical setting is perceptive and brilliant. Similarly, how appropriate it is to set the Palai poems with their essential theme of separation in the dry wilderness, at midday in the hot summer months, with straggling trees and the fierce Kottravai-worshipping highwaymen!

However the mudhal and karu, the first and seed themes, are no mere props. In the poetic technique known as ullurai uvamam or implicit simile they can become extremely suggestive.

This man—
from the village
where the *valai* fish in the wet field
snatches away
a ripe mango falling
beside the field—
has gone back to his son's mother
throwing to the wind
all his promises to me.
He now kow-tows
before that woman
like a puppet
lifting his hands and legs
as she pulls the strings.

(what the concubine said about the husband—the wife's
people overhearing)

Marutam
—Alankudi Vanganar

KURUNTHOKAI 8

In this poem for instance, the *karu* elements of *valai* fish, wet
field and ripe mango signify the hero's easy access to pleasure
and happiness. Such nuances greatly enrich the poems and prove
to be a challenge to the reader.

While only those elements appropriate to the *thinai* could
figure in the poem a certain amount of latitude was permitted
with reference to *karu*. The category of exception was called

thinai mayakkam (ambiguity or overlapping). But the area where no transgression of tradition was brooked was in the uri—the essential theme; the defining element of *akam*; or what made *akam*, *akam*. V.Sp. Manickam goes so far as to argue that the organizing principle for the *akam* anthologies is the uri. Taking up the three major anthologies of *akam* poetry he argues that the long *Akananuru* poems exemplify all the three thematic elements, *mudhal*, *karu* and uri; *Nattrinai* exemplifies *karu* and uri while the shorter *Kurunthokai* is dominated by uri alone.[7]

There are further conventions that make for *akam* poetry. The inviolable rule of *Tholkappiyam* being that 'in *akam* poetry no one may be mentioned by name'. In other words, the dramatis personae may not be identified, and they may be mentioned only by pronouns and in generic terms. The poets therefore do not speak in their individual voice but in and through the various characters as though in a dramatic play. If they do otherwise, then the poem becomes a *puram* poem (e.g. Nakkannaiyar's poem, *Purananuru* 83). The chief protagonists are the heroine and the hero; the girl's friend and the hero's friend; the mothers—biological and foster— of the girl, the concubine and occasionally the hero's charioteer. This stipulation was so normative that a *thinai* fundamentalist like the enormously erudite fourteenth-century commentator Nachinarkkiniyar goes so far as to classify the *Pathupattu* poem *Nedunalvadai* as a *puram* poem despite its overwhelmingly manifest *akam* content because the hero of the poem can be identified as the Pandyan king by his emblematic neem flower! The anonymity of the actors undoubtedly gives the poems a universal quality, communicating across time and space.

It has been suggested that the actors in the *akam* poems come from privileged sections of society—in Kailasapathy's words, the royal and aristocratic echelons. While the *Tholkappiyam* indeed excludes some categories—especially servants and the like—it is evident from the poems that the dramatis personae come from all walks of life. These personae speak in a variety of situations—all marked in the colophons. The union of the lovers; ruminating about the union; discussion with the friend about the desperation of love; approaching the girl's friend for help in carrying forward the love; the setting up of daytime and nightly meetings; the calling of the shaman and soothsayer to cure the malady of the pining girl; the scandalous gossip about the affair; standing steadfast in love in the face of familial opposition; elopement of the lovers; the mother's grief and search for the eloped girl; the husband's separation in search of wealth, education and adventure; the wifely sulking due to the husband's infidelity, etc. In fact, tradition enumerated an elaborate scheme of stock situations in amorous life—a sub-theme of *thinai* called *thurai*. It is within this strict regimen of tradition that the poets had to improvise and display their talent.

A striking aspect of the *akam* poems is how much it is a women's world. The poems revolve so much around women and through them. Of the 1,862 *akam* poems, 785 poems are in the girl's friend's speech; 550 in the heroine's; seventy-two in the mothers' words and the concubine's in fifty-one. The hero and others (other women not excepted) speak in 401. V.Sp. Manickam categorically states that the heroine's father and brother are not permitted to speak.[8] The girl's friend is so pivotal to the situation and so closely identifies herself with the heroine that she often uses the first person plural!

Akam is so central to the corpus and tradition that there is no major Sangam poet who has not written *akam* poems while that is not the case with *puram* poems. Further the word Tamil itself, by extension, came to stand in for *akam*. Interestingly *puram* is a residual category. All that do not fall into *akam* become *puram*. Of the total corpus of Sangam poems only 519, barely one-fourth, belong to the category of *puram*. Despite this relatively meagre crop, these gems, apart from their aesthetic brilliance, continue to be mined for a wealth of historical, anthropological and sociological details.

Like *akam, puram* too is divided into *thinais. Tholkappiyam* lists the following *thinais* which are the counterparts to the *thinais* in *akam*: Vetchi (Kurinji); Vanchi (Mullai); Ulignai (Marutham); Thumbai (Neidal); Vagai (Palai); Kanchi (Perumthinai) and Padan (Kaikkilai). The *mudhal* and *karu* elements are more or less the same but the *uri* pertains to specific *puram* activities. If Vetchi pertains to capturing enemy cattle as a prelude to war, Karanthai is concerned with the retrieval of cattle after the enemy raid. Vanchi is invading the enemy. Ulignai is the encirclement of enemy fortifications. If Thumbai is the waging of war, Vagai celebrates victory in war. Padan talks of the glory of warriors and kings in battle, in charity, in fame and honour. But this *Tholkappiyam* classification of *puram* is expanded by the ninth-century grammar *Purapporul Venpa Malai* to include Nochi (concerned with facing the enemy's onslaught—a constitutive part of Ulignai according to *Tholkappiyam*), Kaikkilai and Perumthinai, both originally poor-cousin *thinais* in *akam*. Pothuviyal is a miscellaneous category encompassing left out themes. In this revised classification, Kanchi, when it doesn't describe war activities—which is not very often—talks of the mutability and transience of life. Especially moving are the elegies written at the death of righteous and brave kings and chieftains. *Purananuru* follows the later division rather than *Tholkappiyam* which greatly annoyed Nachinarkkiniyar!

The thinais are thus explicated but only in the abstract and, as V.Sp. Manickam writes, 'the content and grammar of the puram thinai is not subject to minute definition'.[9] But it cannot be gainsaid that the poets themselves were unaware of the classification: in a brilliant 'meta-fictional' move one poet states that the king, by his many exploits, has exhausted all the thurais.

There are a number of poems describing gruesome wars and battles and the laying waste of enemy lands. The bravery of warriors and young men, not to speak of kings and chieftains, is extolled in great detail. But the pride of place in the puram poems must go to those in Padan and Kanchi thinais. Literary production of the times was underpinned by patronage and we see that the bulk of the poems eulogize the patrons—the kings and chieftains. A special relationship often developed between poet and patron—Kapilar and Pari, and Avvaiyar and Athiyaman are exemplary instances. Despite their dependence on patronage, we find poets siding with minor chieftains against powerful monarchs, refusing largesse when doled out without discernment and not hesitating to proffer good counsel when the patrons took the wrong path. While the bravery and honour of the heroes are glorified in the Padan poems, which account for as many as 139 poems, the Kanchi thinai, with its concern for the mutability and transience of life has a certain universal appeal. (Not surprisingly, M.L. Thangappa's selections are partisan to Kanchi and Padan thinais.)

Composing the Tradition

A striking feature of Sangam poetry is a certain repetitive character which has often been noticed and commented upon by scholars. It is usually explained away by the strictly mandated adherence to *Tholkappiyam*'s dictates, especially with regard to conformity to *thinai* and *thurai* divisions. The repetition has however to do not only with content and themes but also with language. It was not until K. Kailasapathy, the renowned Marxist critic, in his brilliantly written but nevertheless schematic work *Tamil Heroic Poetry*, posed these questions did they receive adequate scholarly treatment.

Especially strong in its comparative sweep, *Tamil Heroic Poetry* drew on the work of the Chadwicks, Milman Parry and A.B. Lord to squarely fit Sangam poetry into the framework of heroic poetry. Through a close textual analysis of the poems, Kailasapathy enumerated and identified the preponderance of formulaic expressions, repetition of stock phrases, noun epithets and lines, ideas and groups of ideas ('it is a continuous process of interlocking expressions—one depending on the other, and ending up in whole formulaic verses'[10]). By analysing this he proposed that the technique of oral verse-making is evident in Sangam poetry and goes so far as to call the Sangam corpus 'bardic poetry', an assertion he repeats often. Kailasapathy's arguments are rather seductive as they explain much of the making of Sangam poetry. The recent recording of the Siri Epic in the Tulu language, which demonstrates the persistence and survival of oral epics in the Dravidian-language-speaking area, by a team of Indian and Finnish scholars, also appears to lend further credence to Kailasapathy's arguments.

While there is no denying the explanatory potential of Kailasapathy's arguments, it far from exhausts the mechanics of composition and raises a number of questions—unanswered and unanswerable. George Hart has raised two very important questions. The oral poetry described and analysed by Lord and Parry is epic poetry; Sangam poetry, on the other hand, consists of a number of individual short poems and therefore does not answer to the criterion of epic poetry. Secondly, and more importantly, there is the complexity of the poems themselves. Drawing on Lord's concept of 'nonperiodic enjambement' which is a technique of a simple adding style characteristic of heroic bardic poetry, Hart points out that the majority of Sangam poems are marked by the literary style of 'periodic enjambement' and are 'so complicated that it takes a detailed commentary for even a reader skilled in the language to determine the exact sense and the precise grammatical function of each clause without painstaking analysis'.[11]

Further questions may be posed. Kailasapathy's point about the lack of writing in the Sangam period is seriously challenged by the numerous graffiti and Tamil Brahmi marked potsherds found all over Tamil Nadu. Considering the stratigraphic levels at which they have been found, and their spread and content, archaeologists and palaeographers have plausibly argued that they demonstrate widespread literacy at the time of the composition of Sangam poems. Further, given the reference to the Vedas as the 'unwritten word' (*elutha karpu, Kurunthokai* 156) it could be argued that it indicates by contrast that Tamil works were indeed written.

Kailasapathy's elaborate classification of bards into *panar* (minstrels), *porunar* (war bards), *kuthar* (minstrels who sing and dance), *viraliyar* (female dancers and singers) and *akavunar* (diviners and soothsayers) who are all distinguished from the *pulavar* (the learned and wise poets), while indeed reflective of the various kinds of literary producers depicted in Sangam poetry, is however not substantiated by the actual literary product. As Kailasapathy himself demonstrates, the corpus, an organic whole with a great deal of homogeneity, is evidently the work of a single class of literary producers, viz., the *pulavars*. It is indeed a strange corpus of heroic poetry where no bards and minstrels contributed!

Kailasapathy further points out that 'originality' is anachronistic in relation to heroic poetry as the primary task of the bard is to improvise in extemporaneous situations. But as we know at least twenty-seven poets are known, named and identified only by a striking image or metaphor or phrase that they have distinctly coined and employed in their poems. If stock epithets and formulaic phrases were everything (which in Kailasapathy's words 'really add very little to the meaning'![12]) we would not have the likes of Chempulappeyanirar ('the poet of rainwater and red soil') and Orerulavanar ('the poet of the single plough'). This also flies in the face of the tradition of praising individual poets for their mastery of individual *thinais* (e.g. Kapilar for Kurinji and Perunkadunko for Palai). Also considering the number of poets across generations who go by the name of Avvaiyar, Nakkeerar and Kapilar, and the famous illustrative example of 'Kapila-Paranar' for the grammatical concept *ummai thokai*, would vouch for the argument that individuality and originality were by no means unknown commodities.

Another point completely missed by Kailasapathy is that some of the best poems in the corpus are the ones with no epithets, stock or otherwise, at all. Let me illustrate with a poem each from *akam* and *puram*.

Keep off, enemies
from the battlefield!
For among us

is a veteran soldier,
strong as a chariot wheel
which a carpenter
skilled to make
eight chariots a day
laboured for a month to shape.

—Avvaiyar on Athiyaman

PURANANURU 87

I am here:
my loveliness
eaten away by pallor
is lost in the woods by the sea.
My lover is comfortable in his hometown.
And the guarded secret of our love
is all over the village square.

(what the girl told her friend, complaining of the lover's
dalliance)

Neidal
—Venputhi

KURUNTHOKAI 97

We find in poems such as these, shorn of epithets or qualifying
phrases, a certain sparseness characteristic of modern poetry. A
Procrustean theory should not blind us to this aspect of a good
part of the Sangam poems.

Continuing the Tradition

The Sangam poems, as we mentioned earlier, were anthologized many centuries later. Evidently, the act of anthologization conferred much prestige on the patron who commissioned the anthology and the scholar who executed it. It is at this time that the invocatory poems, addressed to various Saivite gods, were placed at the beginning of each work. It is likely that the *thinai* and *thurai* classification was provided and colophons added at this point in time.

The availability of a number of mnemonic verses listing the various works of the Sangam corpus along with the authors and contents indicates the establishment of a tradition. This corpus was the subject of much erudite commentary which continues to illuminate (and occasionally obfuscate as well) the poetry. Pride of place must surely go to Nachinarkkiniyar for his commentary of *Pathupattu* and *Kalithokai*. Parimelalagar commentated on *Paripadal*. The old commentators of *Purananuru* and *Ainkurunuru* remain unfortunately anonymous. *Tholkappiyam*, considering that it was a grammatical work, has been the object of much commentary. Seven early commentators explicated it either in full or in part. And the tradition of commentating on it continued in the eighteenth century with Sivagnana Munivar's exegesis of the first *nurpa*.

Akam has been the object of further elaborate grammars: *Tamil Neri Vilakkam* (ninth century),[13] *Iraiyanar Akapporul* (tenth century), *Agapporul Vilakkam* or *Nambi Akapporul* (thirteenth century), *Kalaviyal Karikai* (thirteenth century), *Maran Akapporul* (sixteenth century), etc. Similarly *Purapporul Venpa Malai* (ninth century), which is said to be modelled on the now unavailable *Panniru Padalam* (c. eighth century), explicates the various *puram thinais* and *thurais* in elaborate detail and continues to be the mainstay for an understanding of *puram*.

The literary inspiration provided by Sangam poetry has been fertile. Many of the *thurais* later evolved into separate genres. The genre of Kovai owes its existence to *akam* poetry. Yanai-Maram grew into Parani. The *thurai* of Makatpar Kanchi, which poignantly portrays the devastation visited upon a proud chieftain's clan for refusing to give his daughter in marriage to the royalty flowered into Kalampakam. The theme of the hero threatening to ride the palm-frond horse if the girl failed to reciprocate his love evolved into the genre called Matal. Thus can some of the ninety-six genres of minor literature be traced to Sangam poetry. One of the high points of the continuing tradition was the *Purathirattu*, the anthology of *puram* poems. Compiled in the fifteenth century, this anthology puts together over 1,500 poems on *puram* themes.

The debt of later devotional and didactic literature to Sangam literature, as V.Sp. Manickam points out, 'cannot be overstated'.[14] The third book of *Thirukkural* is *akam* poetry in its distilled essence and aesthetic brilliance. The best of the bhakti poetry of the Alwars and Nayanmars aspire to be *akam* poems. One has only to look at the references in U.V. Swaminatha Iyer's *Kurunthokai* commentary to sample the enormously rich allusions to Sangam poetry replete in the bhakti literature and later works. It is worth noting that Sangam poetry is a source of inspiration to contemporary Tamil poets as well.

Canonizing the Tradition

The story of the recovery of the Sangam classics is the stuff of legend. As we saw above, the Sangam classics were very much part of mainstream literary tradition for about a millennium and a half. Themes from the Sangam classics had evolved into separate genres. Some of the greatest commentaries, brilliantly glossed, carefully elaborated and sometimes argued to hair-splitting extent were written even until the fifteenth century. Conforming to Orientalist stereotypes about decadent indigenous culture at the cusp of colonial rule, the immediate pre-colonial Tamil literary sphere was marked by religious bigotry and sectarianism. The largely secular nature of the Sangam classics coupled with its suspected Jain or Buddhist contamination drew the ire of influential eighteenth-century Tamil scholars like the grammarian Swaminatha Desikar and the commentator-scholar Sivagnana Munivar who forbade their study. Given that mainstream Tamil literary tradition was dominated by the Saiva religion and that Saiva monasteries had a near monopoly over pedagogy and acted as the primary repositories of religious and literary texts, this antagonism to non-Saiva texts had a particularly deleterious effect on the preservation of the Sangam classics. While a few texts such as *Tholkappiyam*, given that it was a grammatical text, survived this sectarianism, the prime Sangam literary texts suffered greatly. From the eighteenth century, at least for a few generations, the Sangam literary texts along with the now venerated classics such as *Silappadhikaram* and *Manimekalai* were all but forgotten. For instance, even Meenakshisundaram Pillai, the greatest of nineteenth-century Tamil teachers, whose life is exceptionally well-documented, is not known to have been familiar with Sangam literature.

Even though Tamil was the first Indian language—in fact, the first non-European language—to use Gutenbergian movable type, as early as in 1577, paper, not to speak of print, was hardly used in the Tamil literary world until the early nineteenth century. Conventionally slats of palm leaves were used as writing material with a sharp metal stylus acting as the pen. In the best of circumstances—storage in a dry place away from dampness, periodic cleaning with turmeric, etc.—palm leaves do not survive long. Reproduction amounted to preservation. Copying of texts, a time-consuming process pregnant with difficulties, by generations of students and scholars alone ensured preservation. Given the large investment in time and resources it demanded, Jain philanthropists hired scribes to copy important texts and gifted them to scholars on festive occasions. In the sectarian climate of the times the palm-leaf manuscripts rapidly disintegrated. Termites, silverfish, fungi combined with indifference and apathy were a fatal cocktail. Certain rituals compounded the problem. During the ninth day of Dussehra when the goddess of learning was honoured, manuscripts were traditionally cleaned and worshipped. On the other hand, old manuscripts that had been copied were never simply thrown away. Either they were dropped in the river on auspicious days (especially the eighteenth day of the month of Adi when the Kaveri was in full flow) or ritually consigned to the flames on the day before the harvest festival of Pongal when the house was cleaned and spruced up. As often happens with rituals when form takes over substance, many as yet uncopied palm-leaf manuscripts were ritually destroyed. Thus did many priceless texts perish. To such mindless rituals must go the blame for many of the missing poems in the Sangam corpus. Apart from the missing poems in the corpus whole commentaries are also lost: Perasiriyar and Nachinarkkiniyar's commentary on the *Kurunthokai* poems must surely head this list.

The social and cultural transformations occasioned by colonialism provided the context for the recovery of texts. A centralized, bureaucratic administration, the establishment of educational institutions based on the Western model, the spawning of new professions, the creation of a new middle-class elite and the development of modern means of communication such as the railways and telegraph, not to speak of the power of print, were factors in the recovery of the texts. It is no coincidence that two of the greatest scholar-editors of the century—C.W. Damodaram Pillai (1832–1901) and U.V. Swaminatha Iyer (1855–1942)—were an official in the colonial administration and a teacher in a government college, respectively.

In 1812 the College of Fort St George, the brainchild of the unsung Francis Whyte Ellis, had been established. Even if the college's search for old texts and their printing did not directly contribute to the recovery and was perhaps only a catalyst, the formulation of the 'Dravidian Proof', as it has been illuminatingly termed by Thomas R. Trautmann in his pathbreaking work on the college, had a definite bearing on the modern career of Sangam literature. In 1784, William Jones had formulated the spectacular theory of languages as belonging to families and the delineation of the Indo-European family of languages which argued that Sanskrit had congenital relations with Greek and Latin and that Sanskrit was the mother of all Indian languages. Countering this view Ellis conclusively demonstrated that the South Indian languages were independent of Sanskrit and belonged to a different family of languages. The outline of this theory, formulated in 1816, was fully fleshed out in all its linguistic and political glory by Robert Caldwell in his classic *A Comparative Grammar of the Dravidian or South-Indian Family of Languages* (1856).

This intellectual proposition was avidly seized by the newly emergent non-Brahmin elite. Given Sanskrit's close association with Brahminical religion and Brahmins in Tamil Nadu, the Tamil language's independence from Sanskrit was underlined by the non-Brahmin elite. The largely secular nature of Sangam literature, the virtual absence of any reference to caste and the values of love, valour and munificence celebrated in the poems were contrasted to the religious and pedantic nature of Sanskrit literature. In the preface to the very first work from the Sangam corpus to see print, *Kalithokai* (1887), C.W. Damodaram Pillai cites it as one example of a Tamil work which owed nothing at all to Sanskrit.

Between 1887 and 1923 all the Sangam classics had been printed: *Pathupattu* (1889), *Purananuru* (1894), *Ainkurunuru* (1903), *Pathittrupathu* (1904), *Nattrinai* (1914), *Kurunthokai* (1915), *Paripadal* (1918) and *Akananuru* (1923). It is now difficult to imagine the enthusiasm with which these works were received when first printed. No wonder this has often been called the Renaissance, drawing on European parallels where an intellectual revolution took place due to the discovery of Greek texts. From native scholars such as Professor P. Sundaram Pillai and T.T. Kanakasundaram Pillai to European Orientalists such as Julien Vinson and G.U. Pope, they were all, to say the least, ecstatic. In a matter of a generation or two, the entire Tamil canon had come to be transformed—Sangam literature along with *Thirukkural* and *Silappadhikaram*, displaced various religious and devotional texts in the canon. The spectacular announcement of the pre-Aryan Indus civilization, in 1924 by Sir John Marshall, greatly enhanced the scholarly and political importance of Sangam literature by highlighting the possibility of it being a Dravidian civilization. Accompanying the rise of Tamil identity politics and the political success of the Dravidian movement, Sangam literature was widely disseminated through print, theatre, platform and cinema. Names from Sangam literature—Maran, Cheran, Chezhiyan, Ilango, etc.—became commonplace in Tamil society. (Amitav Ghosh gets it wrong by at least a decade in his *The Glass Palace*, when a character in 1940s Malaya is named Ilongo.)

The spectacular canonization of Sangam literature and its enormous popular appeal and political import should not detract us from the essentially scholarly and intellectual project it was. The recovery and redaction of the texts was tortuous. In the later half of the nineteenth century many texts were known only in name. The palm-leaf manuscripts, heavily damaged and in complete neglect and disarray, lay scattered in badly maintained monastic libraries and in the lofts of erstwhile pandit families. Making them part with the manuscripts even for perusal and copying was, in the words of C.W. Damodaram Pillai, akin to acquiring the mythical ruby when the black cobra was yet alive. In the event, deciphering the badly damaged manuscripts was no easy task. The orthography employed posed a number of difficulties. As dots, essential to write consonants, could not be used (as they would damage the leaves), a single character could be read in more than one way. Punctuation being absent, letters, words, lines, verses, commentary, glosses and quotations followed one another without breathing space. Reading them demanded a good knowledge of prosody and a vast vocabulary. The unfamiliar vocabulary and syntax of Sangam literature posed apparently insurmountable problems.

This is perhaps the place to state a paradox: after two millennia of their composition, while many poems are direct and simple, almost in everyday language, there are sections which require, and often defy, unlocking even with the aid of insightful commentaries.

The difficulties are in both vocabulary and grammar. Some words, like *andru* and *omputhal*, mean the exact opposite of the current sense. Some grammatical forms are not quite clear. Even after over a century of modern scholarship the final word has not been said on the meaning of much of the texts.

As a rubric in U.V. Swaminatha Iyer's autobiography goes, it was 'a separate universe'. He adds: 'It appeared like another unique language'; 'The vistas of the new world depicted in the Sangam books appeared as the mountains covered by mist. Though this heavy mist hung over the mountains, its loftiness and magnitude though not fully visible was yet perceptible as larger than the earth, vaster than the sky and immeasurably deeper than the seas.'[15]

Translating the Tradition

There has been a long tradition of translating Sangam poetry into English and, to a certain extent, other European languages. It began with the Orientalist interest in Tamil, largely as counterweight to the Sanskrit bias of Indology. Even by the end of the nineteenth century, as the Sangam classics went into print, G.U. Pope had identified *Purananuru* as 'heroic poetry' and had begun to translate from it.

In the post–World War II period American academic interest in India had taken considerable proportions. In the early 1960s A.K. Ramanujan stepped into the scene, accidentally discovering Sangam poetry when he went looking for a book of grammar in the stacks of the Harper Library of the University of Chicago. A slim volume of *Fifteen Poems from a Classical Tamil Anthology* (1965) was followed by the celebrated *The Interior Landscape* (1967) and the more substantial *Poems of Love and War* (1985). The directness of the poems broke the Western stereotypes, based on an exclusive focus on Sanskrit literature, that Indian poetry could only be ornate. A gifted poet himself, Ramanujan brought his considerable skills to make the classics read like contemporary poems. His translations are distinct not only because of his idiosyncratic typographic arrangement which he suggested communicated the syntactic structure of the original poems. His theoretical reflections on translation and his scholarly afterwords to his publications fed into the academic fields of postcolonial and translation studies. His acute dependence on commentaries and some howlers notwithstanding (for instance his mistaking the indigenous hill tribe of *kuravan* for the modern-day *nari-kuruvars* and translating it as 'gypsy', and his literal translation of '*sen-na pulavar*' as 'red-tongued poets'),[16] there's no gainsaying Ramanujan's immense contribution. If Sangam poems are now found in anthologies such as the *Penguin Book of Love Poetry, Penguin Book of Women Poets* and *Women Writing in India*, and even on the London Underground, and more than one novel draws its title from Sangam poems (Vikram Chandra's *Red Earth and Pouring Rain*, P.A. Krishnan's *The Tiger Claw Tree* and Preeta Samarasan's *Evening is the Whole Day*), the credit goes to Ramanujan alone.

A peculiar situation obtains in Tamil Nadu where Tamil works are translated into English in the vain (in both senses of the word) hope that the mere translation into a global language would win worldwide recognition. Not surprisingly such translations are of uneven quality without a sensitive ear to the nuances of idiom and contemporariness. M.L. Thangappa is therefore exceptional. Born (1934) in Kurumpalaperi, a small village in Tirunelveli district not far from the mythical birthplace of Tamil, the Pothikai hills, Thangappa comes from a family of Tamil pandits. Thangappa's father and at least two of his uncles were Tamil teachers. Thangappa was a somewhat precocious child and when barely a boy he could recite scores of Tamil poems. (This immersion in Tamil verse at an impressionable age has had a very peculiar effect on his prosodic skills. His keen ear can always detect minor variations or improvisations in metric forms even when not being able to actually name them.) When Thangappa went to the then venerable St John's College, Palayamkottai, his grasp of idiomatic English, already imbued from reading English fiction, was buttressed by reading the Bible and the Romantic poets taught by learned teachers including European clergymen who lectured there. As a Tamil teacher for over twenty-five years lecturing at various colleges of the Puducherry government, Sangam literature has been the staple of his teaching, parsing and interpreting the terse poems for generations of students.

Thangappa is an accomplished Tamil poet who has published several collections. Not for him free verse, and all his poems are written in a variety of traditional metrical forms. His mastery of Sangam vocabulary and prosody is such that he has even written a modern 'guide poem': *Iyarkai Attrupadai* mimics the *attrupadai* genre to guide an urban youth to the pleasures of nature. Here is tradition encountering talent at its best. He has also written a number of Tamil poems in the *akam* and *puram* genres. Sundara Ramaswamy's words in his novel *J.J.: Sila Kurippukkal* about one Cherthalai Krishna Iyer, 'I could barely even begin to imagine his scholarship in Sangam Literature. I fancied that he could probably go through a novel written exclusively in Sangam vocabulary, as one reads the daily *Dina Thanthi*,' has often reminded me of Thangappa.

It is this thorough immersion in Sangam poetry—its language, vocabulary, style and content—that makes Thangappa an enviable translator. His understanding of the poems is more intuitive than erudite. Not for him the second-hand interpretation of Sangam poems through medieval and modern commentators.

Exactly half a century ago began Thangappa's forays into translation. At the instance of Tha. Kovendhan he began translating poems for his Tamil poetry monthly, *Vanambadi*, and, later, for Perunchithiranar's *Thenmoli*. His earliest translations used traditional English metre and rhyme which he soon abandoned. Selections from his later attempts were published privately in 1970 as a slim volume, set elegantly in italics in a small letterpress in Puducherry. *Hues and Harmonies from an Ancient Land* (with its quaint Shelleyan allusion), H & H for short, already signals his genius for translating Tamil classical poetry. In this phase we can discern his habit of not translating stock epithets and formulaic phrases, and a penchant to explain and paraphrase a bit—a desperate sign of wanting the non-Tamil reader to understand. By the 1980s, when I had begun to work closely with him, he was already moving towards terseness and brevity.

Thangappa's self-effacing nature combined with an indifference to the ways of English publishing has meant that the files of translations in his chaotic study have kept accumulating. It has been said that great works of literature should be translated anew for every generation. In a manner of speaking, Thangappa has done that himself, revising his translations for every generation.

Nabokov listed three unbreakable rules for a good translator: intimate knowledge of the language from which one translates; experience as a writer of the language into which one translates; and 'that one knows, in both languages, the words designating concrete objects (natural and cultural, the flower and the clothing)'. Thangappa fits the bill perfectly. Though his English is not half as good as his Tamil it is saying an enormous lot. Regarding the third of the Nabokovian rules, Thangappa is a nature enthusiast who bicycles long distances and can identify many a flower and plant by its Sangam nomenclature.

Since my encounter with H & H, and my first meeting with Thangappa on a rainy evening at the wedding of Tha. Kovendhan's sons in September 1983, I have had a continuing conversation with him. I have been his student, typist, secretary, PR man, literary agent and collaborator all rolled into one. Reading, interpreting, comparing, composing, editing, circulating his translations, and knocking on the doors of publishers for a quarter of a century has been a rewarding exercise even if it has been often punctuated by frustration. In a sense it has been a dream come true to publish in Penguin, from whose classics series I have read some of the finest translations of the world's greatest writings.

This volume

Love Stands Alone is divided into two sections: Akam and Puram. Translations from Akam, as a rule, have tended to be divided into *thinais*. This book avoids this division. The original Sangam works themselves do not follow this except in the case of *Ainkurunuru* and *Kalithokai*. In any case the poems are not spread equally over the five thinais. Kurinji, with its theme of union in love, and Palai, focussing on separation, take up a lion's share. However, the thinai is stated at the end of the poem but not the thurai.

Kurunthokai makes for the bulk of the selections—not surprising considering that it occupies pride of place, along with Purananuru, in the canon. (A staggering 236 poems of this anthology have been cited in the various early commentaries.) It has received the most critical scholarly attention with a number of editions as well. With its concentrated focus on uri porul with just the right amount of background detail for the proper setting of the thematic matter and an optimum length of four to eight lines Kurunthokai also seems to be eminently suited for translation into English. The result is astonishing: poems written some two thousand years ago read so much like modern poems.

This is followed by selections from Ainkurunuru. These short poems provide the foil for Kurunthokai. Brief selections then follow from Nattrinai, Akananuru and Kalithokai. To give a sampling of the continuing tradition, selections from Ainthinai Aimpathu, Ainthinai Elupathu and Thinaimalai Nuttraimpathu, all post-Sangam works are given.

Titles have been provided for individual poems. Colophons in the original poems are the subject of much debate. The scholarly consensus is that they were composed at the time of anthologization. Some colophons are the contribution of later commentators. The aptness of these has been open to debate. The colophons are sometimes misleading too.

'Coo–coo,' the rooster crows,
and a chill runs through my heart.
Dawn has come

like a cruel sword
to tear me apart
from my lover's arms.

(what the girl said to herself)

Marutam
—Allur Nanmullai

KURUNTHOKAI 157

This brilliant poem is marred by the extant colophon: 'what the wife said at the onset of her menses'! This book, therefore, adapts and summarizes the traditional colophons.

All the selections in the Puram section are from the *Purananuru*. Titles, once again, have been provided. As the poems can stand by themselves, *thinai* and *thurai* have been avoided.

I have followed the 'Murray' editions for names of authors, colophons, etc. There are significant variations in various editions in the names of the poets—especially with regard to the honorific '*ar*' suffix.

Some indispensable notes that help towards a better understanding have been provided at the end of the book. Diacritics have been avoided. Tamil words are spelled as they normally appear in English text in Tamil Nadu.

Fascinated by Thangappa's translations and having, hopefully, internalized his style I tried my hand at translating some Sangam poems in the early 1990s. These translations have had the benefit of Thangappa's revisions. I have thought it not altogether inappropriate to include them in this volume. For the sake of record *Purananuru* 79, 124, 130, 131, 134, 230, 239, 243, 309 and 332, and *Kurunthokai* 32, 112, 130, 131, 138, 206, 290 and 310 are my translations.

Acknowledgements

First thanks go to R. Sivapriya for her enthusiastic reception to our proposal. Whitney M. Cox's careful reading of the penultimate draft along with measured praise and gentle suggestions for minor revisions has greatly helped in finalizing the manuscript. B. Mathivanan and Y. Manikandan, two very perceptive Tamil scholars, helped in various ways by clarifying my doubts. Kesavan Veluthat carefully read and commented on the introduction as did Udaya Kumar. R. Ilakkuvan and M. Arivalagan provided occasional research assistance. A version of the introduction was presented at the department of English, Delhi University, and received useful comments. A. Dakshinamurthy pointed out a few misreadings which have been corrected in this Penguin Classics reprint. Based on Sharanya Manivannan's review the title of a poem has been similarly revised. Arvind Krishna Mehrotra, apart from providing a generous endorsement, ran his fine eye over the poems and suggested revisions that have greatly enhanced their quality. His advice regarding titles was especially helpful.

This book is dedicated to Tha. Kovendhan, M.L. Thangappa's friend and my mentor, who brought us together. What would Kovendhan have not given to see this Penguin book!

Akam

Butterfly with beautiful wings

Butterfly
with beautiful wings,
living by
sucking nectar,
tell me honestly,
is there any flower
known to you
more fragrant
than the tresses of this girl
my most dear friend
who has close-set teeth
and a peacock's
graceful mien?

(what the lover said, addressing the butterfly, the girl overhearing)

Kurinji
—Iraiyanar

KURUNTHOKAI 2

3

Larger than the earth

Larger than the earth,
vaster than the sky,
and immeasurably deeper than the seas
is my love for him
from the hills
where the honeybees make
abundant honey
from the black-stemmed
Kurinji flowers.

(what the girl told her friend about her devotion to her lover)

Kurinji
—Devakulathar

KURUNTHOKAI 3

Like a puppet

This man—
from the village
where the *valai* fish in the wet field
snatches away
a ripe mango falling
beside the field—
has gone back to his son's mother
throwing to the wind
all his promises to me.
He now kow-tows
before that woman
like a puppet
lifting his hands and legs
as she pulls the strings.

(what the concubine said about the husband, the wife's people
overhearing)

Marutam
—Alankudi Vanganar

KURUNTHOKAI 8

Out for any shame

One is desperate
to ride a palm-stem horse,
to wear a wreath of
milkweed buds
and be a laughing stock
of the marketplace.
One is out for any shame
when the blinding passion of love
overwhelms the heart.

(what the lover told the girl's friend)

Kurinji
—Pereyin Muruvalar

KURUNTHOKAI 17

Love's fondness

If it be strength
to shake off love and kindness
and depart in pursuit of wealth
leaving us to languish,
let him be strong.
And let us womenfolk be
fools in our fondness.

(what the girl told her friend on her husband's departure)

Palai
—Kopperuncholan

KURUNTHOKAI 20

A heron's witness

When my lover
wedded me secretly,
there was no witness
but the cheat himself.
If he goes back on his pledge
what can I do?

But there stood a heron
on slender, greenish legs
shaped like a millet's stem
looking for fish
in the shallow stream.

(what the girl told her friend, fearing the lover's dalliance)

Kurinji
—Kapilar

KURUNTHOKAI 25

Like the sweet milk

Like the sweet milk of a cow
spilt on the ground
going to waste
without being sucked by the calf
or collected in a vessel,
the speckled beauty of my complexion
is being eaten away
by the pallor of lovesickness,
neither enjoyed by my lover
nor retained by me.

(what the girl told her friend)

Palai
—Velliveethiyar

KURUNTHOKAI 27

The fire of love

I feel an urgency to get up
and smash things,
to knock and break my head,
to send out violent shrieks
as if in mad frenzy.
This cool night breeze
kindles the fire of love in me.
But this callous village
is sweetly sleeping.

(what the girl told her friend)

Palai
—Avvaiyar

KURUNTHOKAI 28

To ride the palm-frond horse

If one can make out
morning and day,
desolate evenings
and night when the world sleeps,
and daybreak,
then this love is false.

To ride the palm-frond horse
and be mocked on the street
is a shame.
So is living
in separation.

(what the lover said to the girl's friend, about his desperation)

Kurinji
—Allur Nanmullaiyar

KURUNTHOKAI 32

Rainwater and red soil

Your mother and my mother
do not know each other.
Your father and my father
are not related either.
As for you and me,
how do we know each other?
And yet,
like the mingling of rainwater
with red soil,
our hearts have mingled.

(what the lover told his beloved after their first meeting)

Kurinji
—Chempulapeyanirar

KURUNTHOKAI 40

Frustration

My legs
have lost their power.
My eyes
searching, and searching,
have lost their keenness.
Oh, oh, more than the number of stars
in the sky's vast expanse
are the others in this world.

(what the foster mother said to herself after searching in vain
for the lovers who had eloped)

Palai
— Velliveethiyar

KURUNTHOKAI 44

The land of lagoons

Young man—
from the land
of the lagoons
gleaming sapphire-like on the sands
where mulli plants
rich with pollen
bear thorns
resembling a squirrel's teeth—
let me tell you this:
though this birth ends
and another comes
may you be my husband
and I,
the darling of your heart.

(what the wife told her repentant husband about her deep
attachment to him)

Neidal
—Ammuvanar

KURUNTHOKAI 49

Village gossip

The cool blue flowers
of the mulli plants
with curved spikes
travel in the wind
and lie scattered
all over the sand
beside the waters,
like pearls scattered from a broken necklace.

That's what it's like
where your man comes from.
I adore him,
your mother likes him,
and your father approves of him.
The village gossip too is afoot
connecting you with him.

(what the friend told the girl—raising her hopes about
marriage)

Neidal
—Kundriyanar

KURUNTHOKAI 51

Like butter on a rock

Admonishing friend,
it would indeed be well
if I could stop this
as you wish.
But this passion of love
keeps spreading
like butter placed on a rock
under a hot sun
melting before the eyes
of a deaf mute without hands
staring at it helplessly.
It is beyond my power
to stop this.

(the lover answers his admonishing friend)

Kurinji
—Velliveethiyar

KURUNTHOKAI 58

The cripple and honey

A large honeycomb
hangs high on a tree
on the top of a tall hill
where kuthal vines
dance in the breeze.
A cripple
squats under the tree
and gratifies himself
by staring at the honeycomb
and licking his cupped palms.
I am like that cripple.
Though I can't win my lover's heart
I keep looking at him
and fill my heart with joy.

(what the girl told her friend)

Kurinji
—Paranar

KURUNTHOKAI 60

Love begins

Her big, cool eyes
sweet like lotuses
pierced my heart
and made my suffering public.
She is a girl of honeyed speech
and soft, round shoulders.
She scares away the sparrows
from the millet crop
grown along with cotton
in the mountain fields.

(what the lover told his friend)

Kurinji
—Mallanar

KURUNTHOKAI 72

Love's foolishness

Chieftain of the shining mountains
where a tall white waterfall
rumbles down the mountainside
making music like the drums
of the skilful street players,
heed my words:
Falling in love
is something to be condemned.
You make a big fool of yourself
going after an unworthy girl
who cannot recognize goodness when she sees it.

(what the friend told the young man warning him against
falling in love)

Kurinji
—Nakkeeranar

KURUNTHOKAI 78

Love's anxiety

Gently he would stroke
my long and curly hair
and put his arms around me.
'Don't cry,' he would say
as he wiped away my tears.
What has become of him now?

In the hillman's mountain fields
where the millet harvest is over
the lush country beans
have started blooming.
Even in this cold winter
he hasn't come home.

(what she said to her friend about her anxiety over the lover's
absence)

Kurinji
—Kaduvan Mallan

KURUNTHOKAI 82

Winter night

My eyes cannot hold back my tears.
I cannot bear this pain
and the dismal solitude
of this winter night.
Cold showers fall
and the biting winds
blow hard through the rain.
Every time the cow shakes her head
to drive away the buzzing flies
her bells start tinkling.
Could there be anyone else
in this village
who hears that muffled sound?

(what the girl told her friend)

Kurinji
—Venkottran

KURUNTHOKAI 86

21

Fire and water

She is the daughter of a hillman
from the hill folk's hamlet
among the tall mountains
where a pure white waterfall
tumbles down the cliffs
and bubbles up through the crevices.
I met her in the foothills
rich with flowers—
a slim young girl
with broad shoulders.
The water of her gracefulness
has subdued the fire
of my manliness.

(what the lover told his friend)

Kurinji
—Kapilar

KURUNTHOKAI 95

All over the village square

I am here:
my loveliness
eaten away by pallor
is lost in the woods by the sea.
My lover is comfortable in his hometown.
And the guarded secret of our love
is all over the village square.

(what the girl told her friend, complaining of the lover's
dalliance)

Neidal
—Venputhi

KURUNTHOKAI 97

Hanging by the bark

If I fear gossip,
my love will weaken.
And if I let my love go,
all that's left is my coyness.

Friend,
look at my womanhood
sapped of its strength
by my lover.
It is like a broken branch
left hanging by the bark
by a foraging elephant.

(what the girl said to her friend worrying over the lover
wasting time)

Kurinji
—Alathur Kilar

KURUNTHOKAI 112

Rain-soaked water lily

An egret
resembling
a rain-soaked water lily
was looking for prey.
A crab saw him
and panicked.
Like an ox
breaking loose
from the herdsman's tether
he fled into his hole
beneath the screw pine's roots.

Your lover, you know
is from this coastal land.
It is time he stopped
his clandestine visits.
However, you needn't worry for now:
the bangle sellers
have also bangles
of a smaller size.

(what the friend told the girl, allaying her fears)

Neidal
—Kundriyanar

KURUNTHOKAI 117

A tiny little snake

A tiny little snake
white and with beautiful stripes
strikes at an elephant
and knocks him down.
Even so,
this beautiful young girl
with sparkling white teeth
and bangled wrists
has struck me down.

(what the lover told his friend after his first meeting with
the girl)

Kurinji
—Sathinathanar

KURUNTHOKAI 119

Evening has come

This water lily, drooping,
with petals closed
resembles the body
of a green-legged egret.
Evening has come.
Not only evening;
soon, darkness too
will close in.

(the girl speaking to herself)

Neidal
—Orampokiyar

KURUNTHOKAI 122

Will home be sweet?

You say that the wilderness
with its straggling *omai* trees
wearing the desolate look
of a ruined village
and the meandering tracks
of the salt mongers
passing in groups
will be a terrible place.
But tell me:
Will home be sweet to her
in her loneliness?

(what the girl's friend told the lover at the time of his leaving)

Palai
—Palai padia Perunkadunko

KURUNTHOKAI 124

The mocking season

The rainy season
has arrived, cool and fragrant.
It laughs at me
from the rain-fed bushes,
showing its gleaming white teeth
of jasmine buds.
It seems to say:
'Her husband did not care
for her wasting youth
and went in search of riches.
He isn't back home yet.
Who knows where he is?'

(what the girl told her friend about the absence of her husband)

Mullai
—Okkur Masathi

KURUNTHOKAI 126

Wanted!

He could not have
burrowed into the earth
or vaulted the skies
or walked on the seas.
If we search for him
land after land,
town after town,
settlement after settlement
he cannot be missing.

(what her friend told the girl)

Palai
—Velliveethiyar

KURUNTHOKAI 130

The swaying bamboo

A great distance separates me
from the village of my girl,
with large lovable eyes,
and shoulders
shaped like the swaying bamboo.

My heart is desperate
like a peasant
with a single plough
and a field
just wet enough.

O what can I do!

(what the lover said to himself)

Palai
—Orerulavanar

KURUNTHOKAI 131

Work is life

It was he who told us:
'Work is life to men
and men are life
to women at home.'
So do not weep my friend.
He will change his mind
and desist from leaving.

(what the friend told the wife—allaying her fear of separation)

Palai
—Palai padia Perunkadunko

KURUNTHOKAI 135

The big village slept

The big village slept.
I did not,
listening to the sound
of the dark blue flowers that fall
from the tender branches
of the nocchi tree, near our home,
with clusters of leaves
shaped like a peacock's feet.

(what the friend told the girl, the lover overhearing)

Kurinji
—Kollan Alisi

KURUNTHOKAI 138

From the mountain spring

She is a sweet girl
with graceful eyes—
scaring away the parrots from the millet field,
weaving a wreath of lilies
picked from the mountain spring.
I do not know
if she knows it or not,
but my heart is still with her
as I lie here
heaving heavy sighs
like a sleeping elephant.

(what the lover told the girl's friend about his lovelorn heart)

Kurinji
—Kapilar

KURUNTHOKAI 142

Do not despair

Do not despair, my friend.
Your man from the hills
is gentle and caring
and abhors a bad name.
So the pallor of separation
wasting your lovely body
will not stay for long.
It will pass away
like wealth in the hands
of the noble-hearted men of charity
seeking greatness,
knowing full well
that impermanence
is the only permanent thing
in this world.

(what the friend told the girl, allaying her fears)

Kurinji
—Nakkeeranar, son of Madurai Kanakkayan

KURUNTHOKAI 143

O dream

O dream,
though you have woken me
from sweet sleep,
you have brought me
the very picture of my sweetheart
who has a dark complexion,
the lovely line of hair
on her belly
resembling the fine filaments
of the summer's *padiri* blooms,
and who wears ornaments
of intricate workmanship.
And lovers like me
parted from their beloveds
will not chide you.

(what the lover said about a dream he had)

Palai
—Kopperuncholan

KURUNTHOKAI 147

Like a crumbling sandbank

My poor feminine modesty!
It has stayed with me for long
and suffered with me.
But it cannot endure
anymore.
Stretched to the limit
it has crumbled
under my love's
overwhelming passion
like a sandbank
covered with sugarcane plants
displaying white blooms
crumbling under the floods.

(what the girl said to her friend who advises elopement)

Palai
—Velliveethiyar

KURUNTHOKAI 149

Like a motherless egg

People scold me, but
what do they know?
Just as a turtle's hatchling
draws strength from its mother
by looking at her,
I draw mine
from my lover.
If he leaves me
I should waste myself
and wither away
like a motherless egg.

(what the girl said to her friend)

Kurinji
—Killi Mangalankilar

KURUNTHOKAI 152

The inky darkness of the night

Whenever a mountain owl called
or a male monkey
leaped from branch to branch
on the jackfruit tree in our front yard
my heart would tremble.
And now,
his long path lies through the mountains
in the inky darkness of the night.
And I pity my heart.
For it cannot help
travelling to him
along this path.

(what the girl told her friend)

Kurinji
—Kapilar

KURUNTHOKAI 153

Dusk has set in

The cheerful farmers
who went to plough their fields
are returning home,
their seed baskets
filled with fresh flowers.
Dusk has set in.
But no word yet
of my husband's chariot
whose cleft-mouthed little bells,
set in a mould of wax
and shaped in a furnace,
keep tinkling
while crossing barren lands
and passing through the thickets
and bringing my husband home
for the evening's banquet.

(what the wife said to herself)

Mullai
—Urodagathu Kandarathan

KURUNTHOKAI 155

Like a cruel sword

'Coo coo,' the rooster crows,
and a chill runs through my heart.
Dawn has come
like a cruel sword
to tear me apart
from my lover's arms.

(what the girl said to herself)

Marutam
—Allur Nanmullai

KURUNTHOKAI 157

Monsoon rains

Monsoon rains,
coming with a stormy wind,
pouring down copiously
with roaring thunder
which kills snakes
in the mountains,
have you no mercy?
You are powerful enough to cleave asunder
even the great Himalayas.
Why do you harass women
who are lonely and helpless?

(what the girl said to her friend about the monsoon—her
lover overhearing)

Kurinji
—Avvaiyar

KURUNTHOKAI 158

With whose love are you smitten?

With whose love are you smitten,
O sea?
For among the woods of the shore
where like the small-headed goats
from the Pooli land,
seagulls thronged and fished,
your waves kept lashing
against the screw pines
bearing white blossoms
and even in the dead of night
I hear your voice.

(what the girl said)

Neidal
—Ammuvanar

KURUNTHOKAI 163

Misting her blue-lily eyes

Crushing the well-fermented curd
with her tender *kanthal*-shaped fingers,
she wiped them
on her clean sari.
And smoke from frying spice
misting her blue-lily eyes,
she did the stirring
and prepared her sour broth at last.
And when her husband
relished it
calling it delicious,
her face brightened
with a happy smile.

(what the foster mother said to the mother after visiting the
girl's home)

Mullai
—Kudalur Kilar

KURUNTHOKAI 167

Love stands alone

In the desolate, rain-forsaken land
the twisted *kalli*'s pods
open with a crackle
frightening the mating pigeons
with their close-knit downy feathers.

He has left me languishing.
'In search of wealth,' he said.
He did not mind the risks on the way.

If it comes to that,
then in this world
wealth has all support
and love must stand alone.

(what the girl said to her friend)

Palai
—Venputhi

KURUNTHOKAI 174

Cobra's shrunken hood

'Your sweetheart's forehead
has grown pale.
The beauty spots on her skin
have lost their glow.
Her plump, round arms
have become thin
causing her bangles to slip away.
All this is because of you!'
My friend,
Why don't you tell this
to my lover from the mountains
where the *kanthal* stalks
with bright red blooms
beaten up by rain
lie battered and wan on a rock
like a cobra with his shrunken hood
lying limp,
and bring home to him
the run-down state of my body?

(what the girl told her friend)

Kurinji
—Madurai Aruvai Vanikan Ilavettanar

KURUNTHOKAI 185

46

Not his fault

He hails from the land
where among the steep hills
the young one of the mountain goat
sucks its fill of its mother's milk
and gambols on the shady hillside.
He is as firm as a rock.
Not knowing this, I worried about him
needlessly.

(what the girl told her friend about the lover's firmness
of purpose)

Kurinji
—Kapilar

KURUNTHOKAI 187

Where is he now?

The angry sun has cooled
and gone beyond the hills.
Evening has come
with its wistful memories.
Where is he now?
Busy in the work he has taken up?
Doesn't it occur to him
that I'd be pining for his company?
Oh, he does not know how
the cool breeze fanning me
aggravates my pain.
My graceful figure
with the loveliness of a doll
is now wan and pale.

(what the wife said to herself)

Neidal
—Terataran

KURUNTHOKAI 195

Love's way

There was a time when
my friend gave you
bitter neem fruit and
you called it
sweet lump of sugar.
But now she gives you
sweet water
from the ice-cool springs
of Pari's Parambu hill
cooler in this month of Thai
and you call it hot and brackish.
Is this the way
your love has gone?

(what the wife's friend told the erring husband)

Marutam
—Milai Kanthan

KURUNTHOKAI 196

Ends up in thorns

It pains my heart.
Oh, how it pains my heart!
The sweet fresh flower
of the nerunji weed
with tiny leaves
growing wild in dry lands
ends up in thorns.
Likewise
my once sweet lover
has now become
cruel and heartless.
How it pains my heart!

(what the wife told her friend, chiding the erring husband)

Marutam
—Allur Nanmullai

KURUNTHOKAI 202

Sweet as nectar

The words of my dear one
are sweet as nectar.
So are her virtues.
But if they can cause such sorrow,
those with some sense
better keep away from love.

(what the lover said to his friend)

Kurinji
—Aiyur Mudavan

KURUNTHOKAI 206

Like foam

'Suffer love,'
they say.
Either they do not know love
or they are brave.

If I don't get to see him,
I with my heavy heart will cease to be,
by slow degrees,
like foam
when running water
splashes against the rocks.

(what the girl said to her friend)

Neidal
—Kalporusirunuraiyar

KURUNTHOKAI 290

Culprits go free

It was in the woods by the seashore
where the hoary sea
plays on the beach
and the birds are clamorous,
that our tryst was agreed upon—
by the dunes
under the laurel tree
blossoming in clusters.
And when I met him there
were it not my eyes that saw him
and ears that took in his words?
But how is it, my friend,
that my arms glow with beauty
when he holds me,
and become blanched and thin
when we part?

(what the girl told her friend, the lover overhearing)

Neidal
—Venmani Puthi

KURUNTHOKAI 299

The sky too is dizzy

The birds have come to roost.
The flowers have closed their petals.
The woods by the shore
are desolate.
The sky too is dizzy
like me.
The day is past
and light has faded.

Friend,
if you could get this across to him,
who is of the littoral land
rich with cool *gnalal* flowers
I shall yet live.

(what the girl said to her friend)

Neidal
—Perunkannan

KURUNTHOKAI 310

The sun and the *nerunji*

Like the rising moon
reflected in the sea
looks the silver waterfall
cascading down the mountain
in the land of my beloved.
He is like the sun
and my shapely arms
are like *nerunji* flowers.

(what the girl told her friend about her devotion to her lover)

Kurinji
—Madurai Velathathan

KURUNTHOKAI 315

Flourescent as moonlight

The fishermen of the high seas
brought home an abundant catch;
and along with shrimps
caught in the inlets
they spread them to dry
on the white sands
fluorescent as moonlight.
The foul smell filled the air
over the dunes
in the seashore land of my lover
with whom I did not spend
even a single day of happiness.
Yet, this heartless village,
surrounded by laurel trees
blossoming in golden clusters
swarming with humming bees,
is rife with malicious gossip.

(what the girl told her friend, the lover overhearing)

Neidal
—Thumbiser Keeran

KURUNTHOKAI 320

Dark as mango shoots

The land has dried up.
Bamboos wilt in the sun.
Dacoits with bows
kill wayfarers
and share the spoils.
Ill-tempered elephants roam everywhere.
But rest assured, my friend,
your husband surely
will not face those dangers
in his search for wealth.
And your complexion
dark as mango shoots
will not become pale.
I know he does not value wealth
more than you.

(what the friend told the wife allaying the fear that her
husband would leave in search of wealth)

Palai
—Vadapiramanthan

KURUNTHOKAI 331

Like a marsh lily

How could you keep visiting her by night
like this,
chieftain of the seashore land,
gladdening the hearts
of your ill-wishers
but making your sweetheart suffer?
Like a marsh lily
crushed beneath the wheels
of a speeding chariot,
its tinkling bells sounding
a plaintive note,
she is already crushed
by your cruelty.

(what the girl's friend told the lover by way of warning)

Kurinji
—Kundriyan

KURUNTHOKAI 336

Chieftain of the mountain land

Chieftain of the mountain land
where waterfall from an awesome cliff
rumbles down the hill
making sweet music like a drum
among the jackfruit trees
growing on the flanks of the hill,
listen:
Your sweetheart is wasting away.
Her bangles made of conch shells
slip off from her thinning arms.
And her eyes, as she looks at them,
are filled with tears,
and she has not a wink of sleep.

(what the friend told the lover)

Kurinji
—Madurai Nalvelli

KURUNTHOKAI 365

Blue lilies of the spring

Marriages are preordained.
Who are we to judge the worth of the groom?
Rejecting the soothsayer's words
your daughter sits gazing
at the blue lilies of the spring
with a heavy heart
and tearful eyes.
Her choice isn't wrong.

(what the girl's friend told the suspicious foster mother)

Kurinji
—Perichathan

KURUNTHOKAI 366

Pledge

He fondled lovingly
your flowing hair
and made his pledge.
'Sweetheart,
when you become mature enough
you will adorn my home.'
He came from the hills
where a hunter digging for roots
finds a precious stone.
I do not know, friend,
where he is now.

(what the girl's friend told her, her parents overhearing)

Kurinji
—Anon.

KURUNTHOKAI 379

Like wax on fire

Friend,
he was in our home
for only a day.
For just that
I've been weeping
all these seven days
melting away
like wax on fire.

(what the girl told her friend)

Marudam
—Orampokiyar

AINKURUNURU 32

The herons have come

The herons have come
to settle on the *marudu* trees
overlooking the fields.
A banquet of fish from fields,
mirrored in the pond's blue waters,
awaits them.
And you hail from that land, my husband.
The new women you are feasting on
are clean and fresh.
Only I appear like a ghost to you
now that I have borne you a child.

(what the wife told her erring husband)

Marudam
—Orampokiyar

AINKURUNURU 70

Milk and honey

The muddy water from a stagnant pool
in his land
which drinking deer had stirred up
was far sweeter to me
than the milk and honey here.

(what the girl told her friend, back home after a brief period
of elopement)

Kurinji
—Kapilar

AINKURUNURU 203

Golden blossoms fill the pit

Mother,
the truth is this:
far away is the mountain
of our chieftain.
The jungle folk
dig out tubers
and leave the pits open.
Golden blossoms
from the *vengai* trees
fill the pits to the brim.
Whenever that mountain
is hidden from view
the flower-like eyes
of your daughter
fill with dew.

(what the friend said to the foster mother)

Kurinji
—Kapilar

AINKURUNURU 208

A jackfruit falls

Look at your lover
planning to fly
to his native land
leaving you
to melt away in tears.
He is from the mountains
where sometimes
a jackfruit falls
into a narrow rift in the rock
destroying the tender honeycomb on a tree.

(what the friend told the girl, her lover overhearing)

Kurinji
—Kapilar

AINKURUNURU 214

Like a golden rope

It was indeed sweet
to think of your virtues, dear,
while I was in the wilderness
where a forest fire spread
looking like a gliding
golden rope
with which the rich
tie their elephants.

(what the husband told his wife after his return from
an assignment)

Palai
—Odhalanthaiyar

AINKURUNURU 356

Tipping the crow

Spotless feathered little crow,
I will treat you
and your loving kin
to a feast of fresh meat and fat
served on a plate of gold.
Come, make your call of good omen
so that my daughter,
with her beautiful locks of hair,
and her hot-headed young man,
with his warrior's spear
with whom she has eloped,
may come back home.

(what the mother said, addressing a crow)

Palai
—Odhalanthaiyar

AINKURUNURU 391

A happy state

He embraced his baby son
and the son's soft-spoken mother
embraced both of them.
What a happy state is theirs!
Not all the world could ever be
as blessed as that.

(what the foster mother told herself while visiting the
daughter in her home)

Mullai
—Peyanar

AINKURUNURU 409

Reminders

The peacock's dancing steps
reminded me of your gait.
The jasmine flowers unfolding
bore the sweet scent of your forehead.
The timid glances of a deer
were like your own glances.
And my heart was filled with thoughts of you.
So I hurried back to you,
swifter than the tempest clouds.

(what the husband told his wife on his return from afar)

Mullai
—Peyanar

AINKURUNURU 492

The bees are singing

The bees are singing on the flowers.
The frogs are croaking their choruses.
In the cool, fragrant pasture lands
jasmine blooms are unfolding.
What a sweet hour it is!
So I have come to meet you, dear.
No more woes for you.

(what the husband told his wife on his return from an
assignment)

Mullai
—Peyanar

AINKURUNURU 494

A man of his word

My beloved
is a man of his word.
The very thought of him brings joy to me.
His love is without blemish
and pure as honey
collected from lotus flowers
and stored in a honeycomb
high on a sandalwood tree.
Knowing full well that
even as the world cannot
live without water,
I cannot live without him,
he soothes me with gracious words.
And he fears to see my bright forehead
stricken with pallor.
Will he stoop so low
as to think of parting?
No, he will not.

(what the girl told her friend, defending her lover)

Kurinji
—Kapilar

NATTRINAI 1

Like tender young turmeric

It was a pleasure
to stay in the fishing village
beside the waters,
where they spread to dry
under the laurel trees
shrimps caught in the inlets,
with their segments
looking like tender young turmeric.
It is no longer so,
for I can no more look
into the gazelle eyes
of the daughter of the fisherfolk,
my girl with slender waist and
broad hips.

(what the lover said to himself)

Neidal
—Velliyanthinnanar

NATTRINAI 101

The ripe hour

The rains have started
helping people
with their work on the land.
On the river bed
the black sand lies silk-soft.
The patterns on it
mimic a serpent's belly.
The lusty mango trees
are aflame with shoots.
Cuckoos perch on them
singing their mating songs.
Stirred by these songs, my beloved
will think of me
and cry with a heavy heart,
the golden speckles
on her brownish body
like pollen lying scattered
from the *vengai* blossoms
beside the narrow rocks.

(what the lover said to himself)

Palai
—Ilavettanar

NATTRINAI 157

What is wealth?

Young man,
hailing from the country
where the peasants who go
to plough their wet fields
soon after the harvest
to sow seeds for the next crop
return home with their seed baskets
filled with fish,
heed my words:
It is not wealth
to gain renown
and to drive in fast-moving chariots,
these are but the result of past deeds.
What the sages call wealth
is a gentle sensitiveness
to the pain and suffering
of those who are close to us.

(what the girl's friend told the erring husband)

Marutam
—Milaikilan Nalvettanar

NATTRINAI 210

Enough courtship

Lovelorn young man,
whenever you watch the birds
coming to roost
or see lovers united
in a close embrace
you heave hot wistful sighs
which resemble the breathing
of a sleeping elephant.
I am sure
your distress is deep.
But your girl is no longer free
to meet you.
Perhaps you have heard of Pari
who pours out and shares rich drinks?
He rules over a lush green hill
where rain clouds ceaselessly
burst into showers
and peals of thunder
rend the air.
Even as that hill is guarded
by an impenetrable forest,
so is your sweetheart
by watchful eyes.

(what the girl's friend said to the lover—to end the courtship
and think of marriage)

Kurinji
—Kapilar

NATTRINAI 253

When the waters receded

When the waters receded
from the creek,
hosts of storks
came down to feast on the lusty fish
in the slushy bed,
and perched on the dunes.
They moved about
like the king's soldiers,
brightly attired.
Go, my friend,
and tell my lover
living beyond the creek
that I am wasting away.
And like the holders of the cattle raided
by the king of Mullur
my loveliness is lost.

(what the girl's friend said to the lover's friend)

Neidal
—Kapilar

NATTRINAI 291

Things will improve

My shoulders are sagging.
My complexion
has lost its glow.
The look of freshness
is gone from my limbs.
You feel mortified, friend,
that you have caused all this.
But there need be no remorse.
My sorrow is deep indeed.
But things are not going
to end like this.
In my lover's mountains,
the raindrops are beautiful
glistening on the
large plantain leaves.
I will win his love
in the end.

(what the girl told her friend, asking her not to worry)

Kurinji
—Kapilar

NATTRINAI 309

I hear the ocean's ceaseless roar

I hear the ocean's ceaseless roar.
The chill wind howls among the trees of the shore.
And in the wide, sandy streets of the village,
an owl perched with his mate
by the village square
lets out his heart-chilling hoots.

Now is the midnight hour of silence
when the spirits are on the prowl.
The stars themselves are at rest.
But I cannot get a wink of sleep.
I think of the sweet embraces
of my girl,
her tender, rounded arms
and her golden spotted breasts.

(what the lover said to himself, pining for his sweetheart)

Neidal
—Vinaitholil Chokeeranar

NATTRINAI 319

The bears come in crowds

A wild boar
with a rough and bristling coat
and his mate
with flabby teats
browsed greedily
in the millet-fields.
A hillman saw them
and crouched for them
in a cave by the path.
He killed the boar
with his arrows.
Later, in the village
the hunter's dark-haired wife
distributed pork
among her kinsfolk.
These are the mountains
from where you come.
You may not be afraid
of the night's treachery,
or of the jungle and the river bed,
where an angry tusker waits
to fight a tiger.
Only I am afraid

for your safety.
For along the narrow mountain path
there are many termite hills
and the bears come in crowds
to dig them up.

(what the girl said to the lover anxious for his safety)

Kurinji
—Kapilar

NATTRINAI 336

In constant terror

The cliffs are jutting out
on the mountain
where clouds come and play—
like bundles of cotton thread
spun by spinsters.
Jackfruits hanging
from the crooked trunks
of the twisted old trees
are large and pot-like.
The hill folk are ploughing
the rocky soil for a living.
The playful daughter of a hillman
is feeding jackfruit
to a black-fingered monkey.
Hailing from these mountains,
young man, you are an adept in love,
but you are not a worthy man.
You keep my friend
in constant terror
for your safety.
For the paths by which you cross the hills
in the dead hours of night
are fraught with danger.

For an elephant
having trampled a tiger to death
trumpets in rage
like thunder.

(what the girl's friend said to the lover asking him not to
make the girl anxious)

Kurinji
—Kapilar

NATTRINAI 353

Scaring away the parrots

I was in the mountain fields
scaring away the parrots.
You made a swing for me
under the *vengai* tree.
You brought me a garment
woven of fresh leaves.
Many are the days on which we met
and many were the joys we shared.
Is there anything sweeter to me
my dear,
than such happiness?
Now my mother
has become suspicious.
Did she notice
the strange fragrance on my hair,
or the lovesick pallor on my face?
She said nothing.
But she sighs to herself now and then
and finds excuses
to keep me in the house.
Our clandestine meetings
must end.

(what the girl said to her lover—asking him to end the
courtship and hasten marriage)

Kurinji
—Kapilar

NATTRINAI 368

The antelopes

The monsoon has arrived.
The heavy rain clouds
bursting into copious showers
have made the forest beautiful.
The pretty *poovai* flowers
have bloomed like sapphire gems.
Many are the red-coated *muthai*
that flit among them.
Pure jasmine flowers withering,
lie scattered everywhere.
With all this, the pastoral landscape
looks like a beautiful painting
by an expert painter.

But, driver, don't drive so fast,
slow down the horses to a trot.
Don't press your spikes too hard
but guide them gently—
our well-trained horses
galloping in rhythmic strides—
for now is midday, the mating hour
of the antelope, whose twisted horns
resemble the bare stem
of the plantain flower
when all the segments have been removed,
and his mate with well-shaped legs.

We should not scare them
with the sound of our chariot
and the fast-moving horses.

(What the husband said to the driver of his chariot)

Mullai
—Sithalai Chathanar

AKANANURU 134

The wedding day

It was our wedding day.
With limitless hospitality
our folks entertained the worthy guests
serving rice cooked with meat and ghee.

Choosing the auspicious hour
when the moon
brightening the sky's vast expanse
and the star Rohini
came together,
they decorated the house
and offered prayers to the gods.
Wedding drums and other larger drums
started playing.
My girl was given her bridal bath,
and the women who bathed her
stood gazing at her form
with wide open, wonderstruck eyes.
And then they departed.

Wearing an amulet
made of the forked leaves,
which have dull undersides,
of the soft-flowered *vagai*
and leaves of *arugu*,
growing wild in pits
browsed by mature calves,

and the sweet-smelling buds of *pavai*,
that sprouted in the first monsoon rain
that came with thunder,
whose petals of blue resemble
neatly washed sapphire stones,
bound together with a white thread,
she looked resplendent and lovable
in her wedding dress.

And under the wedding pandal
spread with fresh, cool sand
her people gave her in marriage to me,
fanning away the perspiration
caused by heavy ornaments.

When we met on our bridal night, I said,
'Darling of my soul, with spotless loyalty,
wrapped in your crisp wedding clothes
you are sweating profusely.
Just push back your veil a little.'
So saying, I pulled at her veil
with a palpitating heart.
And lo! Like a sword out of its sheath
her beauteous, clothe-less form shone brightly.

Not knowing how to cover herself
she bent her head bashfully
and throwing off her garland of water lilies,

she brought down her long tresses of hair
which still had bees swarming
over the fresh flowers worn on them,
and she hid herself behind their darkness.

(what the husband said to himself, unable to bring around his
sulking wife)

Marutam
—Vittrutu Mutheyinanar

AKANANURU 136

Home thoughts

Driver, be quick!
Let us reach home before nightfall.
My wife, poor girl,
will be waiting,
holding her bright bangles
from tinkling,
and gazing frequently down the street
from our well-guarded mansion
with grief in her heart.
She will now be telling her girlfriend
'My darling husband—
riding his chariot
the driver holding the reins
the horses swift like the wind
galloping
breathing hot air
snorting like the bellows
in a blacksmith's forge
with froth at their mouths
like foam on milk when churned
its tiny droplets scattering
like cobweb threads
some of them staining
my husband's chest smeared with sandal paste
the chariot passing
through the pastoral land
cooled by fresh air
and wearing a new look

swift-footed deer
fleeing in fear
of the wheels
with rotating spokes
tearing through the sand
making a noise
that resembles the sound
of the grindstone
when the housewife grinds
dried rice in it—
will soon be home.

(what the husband said to his friend on finishing his work)

Mullai
—Perunthalaichattanar, son of Aavur Kilar

AKANANURU 224

Where will the pallor go?

Our king has won!
His banner of victory is unfurled.
The triumphant drums of war,
thundering from the camp
where the frenzied elephants
are still in a nasty mood,
resound across the battlefield.
The cowherds have started
playing their flutes.
The herded cattle
with their young ones
are sent bounding
across the pasture lands.
Your servants are already
hurrying home.
The driver of your chariot
has a tough time
restraining the horses
galloping madly homewards,
manes flying.

How handsome you look, my chief,
sweet-smelling sandal paste
smeared on your garlanded breast,
adorned with battle scars,
adored by poets!

And when you decide
to return home
with triumphant joy
to meet your wondrous wife
whose eyes with blackened lashes
glitter like blue lily buds,
where will it go—
the lovesick pallor
on her sweet forehead?

(what the servants told the husband, their master)

Mullai
—Madurai Tamila Koothan Kaduvan Mallanar

AKANANURU 354

Spring has come

The mango trees have put forth
sweet young leaves.
The cuckoos on them have started singing
in many voices their dulcet notes.
The blossoming branches have shed their old leaves
and the bees on them
are producing wondrous music as if played
by an adept from a stringed instrument.
Spring has come,
the season in which lovers
forget their homes and
make love in shady groves
where on the white dunes
by the crystalline pools
pollen dust is raining.
Come friend,
let us go into a sulk,
telling him,
'It doesn't become you
to leave me here all alone
without any compassion
and go in search of gold,'
showing him how
my bangles don't stay on my wrists
thinned with grief.

(what the wife said to her friend resenting her husband's
intention to seek wealth)

Palai
—Thankal Mudakottranar

AKANANURU 355

Will he wipe away my tears?

My large, beautiful eyes
that brim with tears
resemble dark blue water lilies
drenched in rain.
How nice it would be, my friend,
if he returns home
to wipe away these tears.
He, who had left me languishing
and passed through a sun-beaten,
waterless stretch of wilderness
where the narrow, fire-eaten tracks
are without any shade,
where a stag,
his forked antlers resembling a barren tree
wanders after mirages
shimmering like blue sands
and with a desolate and weary heart
calls to his mate grazing somewhere else.
His feeble cry
sounds human to the passers-by,
where vast stretches of millet fields
on the mountainside
are bordered by *gnemai* trees with shapely trunks,
where swaying stalks of bamboo
rub against one another and produce screeching sounds
and where even the mountain cliffs are parched.

(what the girl told her friend, pining for her lover)

Palai
—Ilankeeranar, son of Eyinandai

AKANANURU 395

The monk and the mother

'Revered monk,
carrying an umbrella
to shelter you from the sun,
balancing a hermit's jug
on a string from your shoulder
and wielding a three-pronged staff,
on a pilgrimage
with a deep meditative mind,
you are here
having crossed many an arid land.
Did you see on your way
a young girl, my daughter,
and with her, a young man,
both in deep love with each other?'

'I won't say I haven't seen them.
For I saw them in the wilderness.
You seem to be the mother of that girl
fleeing with that fine young man
braving the desert.
Let me tell you:

'The scented sandalwood is born of the hills.
But of what use is it to the hill itself?
It delights only those who smear its paste.
Even so, your daughter.

'The priceless white pearl is born of the seas.
But of what use is it to the sea itself?
It pleases only those who wear it.
Even so, your daughter.

'The stirring notes of music are born of the *yal*.
But of what use are they to the *yal* itself?
They delight only those who play it.
Even so, your daughter.

'Do not think of intercepting
your girl of spotless virtue.
She has chosen for herself
a worthy husband.
This is the law of life
which swerves not from righteousness.'

(A conversation between a monk and the foster mother of
the girl)

Palai
—Palai padia Perunkadunko

KALITHOKAI 9

The bully as lover

Hear this story, friend:
Mother and I were at home.
A stranger came to the door
asking for a drink of water.
Mother said,
'Pour him water
from our jug of gold.'
I went and poured water for him.
Abruptly
he grasped me by the wrist.
Shocked, I cried,
'Mother, see what he is doing!'
Then I knew.
It was he—
the bully of our younger days
who used to tease us
by trampling on our sandcastles,
plucking the garlands from our hair
and running off with our playthings.
But alarmed at my cry
mother came running.
What could I do?
I lied to her:
'This fellow just hiccupped
while drinking the water.'
My credulous mother
began to massage his back.

Love Stands Alone

And that rascal
looking piercingly at me
out of the corner of his eyes
winked and smiled.

(what the girl told her friend)

Kurinji
—Kapilar

KALITHOKAI 51

The cruellest hour

The sun descends into the caverns of the darkening
    western hills
drawing the day into his mouth of receding rays
with which he lit up heaven and earth in the morning.
Darkness overhangs and waits
like the black-complexioned god of the deadly battle wheel.
As the beautiful moon begins to climb the vault of blue,
lotus petals begin to close like eyelids drooping in slumber.
Trees with their bending boughs appear like worthy men
who hang their heads in modesty on hearing praise.
Pearly buds unfold in the dark green foliage,
looking as though the bushes are grinning.
The humming notes of the honeybees flow to match
the music of the cowherds' flutes.
The birds come flying to their roosts.
The cows are hurrying back from pasture, longing for their
    calves.
And all other animals reach their habitations.
The priests welcome the evening with the chanting of hymns.
Torch in hand, graceful maidens light the lamps
    in their homes.
Thus comes the twilight hour
which the naïve call evening.

But it is really the cruellest hour that has come
to torment lovesick girls in their loneliness.

(what the girl told her friend)

Neidal
—Nallanduvanar

KALITHOKAI 119

Dark clouds and pale shoulders

Peacocks
beautifully coloured
make their calls
and as though in answer
thunderclouds
roll and rumble.
Heavy with rain
they sweep down
and hover upon the hills.
Whenever I look at those clouds
my shoulders become pale
with green-sickness.

(what the lonely wife said to her friend)

Mullai
—Maran Poraiyanar

AINTHINAI AIMPATHU 2

Is there no monsoon?

Friend
with sparkling teeth
that put jasmine buds to shame,
tell me:
in that distant land
where my husband has gone,
is there no monsoon season
to display on the sky
killer weapons such as
rumbling clouds, lightning
and peals of thunder?

(what the wife said to her friend)

Mullai
—Maran Poraiyanar

AINTHINAI AIMPATHU 3

Dangers on your path

Young man,
last night your girl
didn't have a wink of sleep
thinking of the dangers
on your path,
where a wounded elephant
with ears folded
walks with stealthy steps,
afraid that the tiger
that had attacked him
might charge again.

(what the girl's friend said to the lover)

Kurinji
—Maran Poraiyanar

AINTHINAI AIMPATHU 16

She belongs to you

Now that the millet crop
is harvested
and the field itself ploughed in,
the parrots and we (who scare them away)
will not visit the fields any more.
But young man
from the mountains
with tumbling waterfalls,
let not your friendship
end here.
The sweet girl belongs to you.

(what the girl's friend said to the lover)

Kurinji
—Maran Poraiyanar

AINTHINAI AIMPATHU 18

Like the bloodstained claws

Like the bloodstained claws
of a tiger,
the season's murukku buds have unfolded.
The cool rain clouds
have disappeared.
Spring has come
making everyone else rejoice.
Only my lonely heart
is filled with grief.

(what the girl told her friend, her lover overhearing)

Palai
—Maran Poraiyanar

AINTHINAI AIMPATHU 31

Evening holds sway

The cowherds
playing their konrai flutes
are on their way home.
Their herds of cattle
walk behind them
thinking of their little calves.
The evening has come to hold sway.
The clouds
burst into peals of thunder
and in front of my eyes
cover the sky
with a rainbow.

(what the girl said to her friend about her loneliness)

Mullai
—Moovathiyar

AINTHINAI ELUPATHU 22

In the pasture land

In the pasture land
beautiful with
rocks standing out
where mullai and talavam
bloom in the bushes,
and where all night
the monsoon clouds
were pouring down
copious showers
on the hillocks,
my black-dyed eyes
were shedding
lonesome tears
on my breasts.

(what the wife said to her friend, grieving about her loneliness)

Mullai
—Moovathiyar

AINTHINAI ELUPATHU 24

Smitten with beauty

Bathing and swimming
in the milk-white waterfall,
she keeps watch
over the *aivanam* field
that looks as though
strewn with many-coloured flowers.
And there is no need for her
to send her spear-like looks
to pierce my heart
and strike me dead with love.
For the moment I set my eyes on her
I was smitten with the beauty
of her graceful form.

(what the lover said to the girl's friend)

Kurinji
—Kanimethaviyar

THINAIMALAI NUTTRAIMPATHU 19

PURAM

A great conqueror

Your swords
stained with the blood
of your enemies
bear the beauty
of the evening sky.

The warrior's anklets
worn around your legs
resemble the tusks
of a killer boar.

Your shield
riddled with arrows
looks like a target board.

Your war horses
grinding their metal bits
and spitting blood
look like tigers
with the victim's blood
in their mouths.

Your elephants
their white tusks broken
battering enemy doors open
look like Death.

Your self
seated on your golden chariot
drawn by swift horses with bright manes flying
have the beauty of the rising sun.

And like a child
who has lost its mother
the lands of your enemies
who have angered you
send out wails and screams
without cease.

—Paranar on Ilanchetchenni

PURANANURU 4

Your land, O king

Your land, O king,
is a stronghold of forests
where wild elephants
roam like grazing cattle
amidst boulders
black and buffalo-shaped.
Since you are the ruler,
let me tell you this:
Do not seek the friendship
of loveless, uncompassionate people
suffering eternal perdition,
but protect your country
as a mother would
her child.
For yours is a position
not easily attained.

—Nariveruuthalaiyar on Cheral Irumporai

PURANANURU 5

Greater than the sun

Aspiring to unsurpassed glory
he resented
sharing the world
with other rulers.
Ambition driven
to expand his kingdom
which he felt was small,
he marched ahead
and conquered territories
with a mighty army.
Even as his will was undaunted
so was his charity boundless.
Such was Cheraladan.
How can you compare with him,
fast-moving orb of heaven?
Your realm is limited.
You back away when the moon comes up.
You hide behind the hills.
And for all your glory
spread across the sky,
you only hold sway
during the day.

—Kapilar on Cheraman Kadunko Valiyathan

PURANANURU 8

Is it right?

The minstrels have received
medallions of gold,
lotus shaped;
and the poets,
elephants
with beautiful foreheads
and decorated chariots.
Is this right, O Kudumi
of glorious victories,
that by taking away
your enemies' lands
and incurring their displeasure
you have made your friends happy
with your gifts?

—Nettimaiyar on Mudukudumi Peruvaluthi, the Pandyan king

PURANANURU 12

Conquests and sacrifices

Razing down the fortressed city
of your enemies
you ploughed up their royal avenues
with donkeys.
Their fertile fields
where birds sang sweetly
you ruined
by driving your horse-drawn chariots
through them.
And their freshwater fountains
you destroyed
by sending your elephants
to trample upon them.
Your anger was so great.
And many were the foes you subdued
who had risen against you
wielding terrible spears
and shields driven with nails
but were unable to stand before your vanguard.
Deprived of all their ambitions
they lived ill-famed lives.

Many also were the sacrifices of fire
you performed
with all the rites and rituals
and oblations of rice cooked with ghee
following sacred books and scriptures.

And of these two acts
which added to your glory most
O king, whose valour deserves
the encomiums sung by the dancing girl
accompanied by well-tuned *mulavu*?

—Nettimaiyar on Mudukudumi Peruvaluthi, the Pandyan king

PURANANURU 15

The whole world fears for your safety

The depth of the dark oceans
the width of this vast earth
and the extent of the earth's atmosphere
can be measured.
But O king,
your intelligence, your compassion
and your generosity can never be measured.
People who live under your canopy
know no other fire
than the fire of the burning sun
and the fire of the cooking stove.
They know no other bow
than the rainbow.
And no other weapon than the plough.
Putting down your powerful foes
you have consumed their soil
but your own soil
is never consumed by anyone else
except pregnant women
who have morning sickness.
Your fort stands against arrows.
Your sceptre stands for righteousness.

In spite of new ill omens appearing
and old ill omens receding
your land is the safest haven for your people.
You are such a noble ruler
the whole world fears for your safety.

—Kurunkoliyur Kilar on Mantharancheral Irumporai, the
Chera king

PURANANURU 20

Marching from land to land

Just as the concepts of wealth and love
come after the concept of virtue,
the canopies
of the other two monarchs
come behind yours
in your triumphal march.
Your reputation shines high like the full moon.
Bent upon winning fame
you never move away
from your battle camps.
Your untiring elephants
attacking enemy forts have blunted tusks.
Your battle-loving soldiers
never refuse to go to war.
They don't complain
that the enemy lands
are far away
and lie across jungles.
Closely watching you
marching from land to land
celebrating your victories
and your war horses
traversing

from the east coast to the west
the northern kings
are terror-stricken
and spend sleepless nights.

—Kovur Kilar on Nalankilli, the Chola king

PURANANURU 31

The sound of the falling trees

Whether you will go to war
or not,
I leave to your judgment.
But your soldiers
entering your enemy's land
have started cutting the trees
of his tutelary forest
with long-handled axes
sharpened with the blacksmith's file.
Tottering under their thrust
the long boughs shed
their sweet-smelling flowers.
The dunes of Aanporunai—
where young maidens
wearing anklets and bangles
used to play *kalangu*
with coins of gold—
are undermined.
The sound of the falling trees
reverberate through the castle gates
and reach your opponent's ears.
Still he keeps blissfully inactive
without a mind to fight you.

Shame on you
that you are here
with the beating of your drums
decked with rainbow-like wreaths
to fight such a coward!

—Alathur Kilar on Killivalavan, the Chola king

PURANANURU 36

A small strip of land

Powerful, victorious and kind,
ruler of a country
where a small strip of land
wide enough for one elephant to lie down
produces enough food
to feed seven war elephants.
You are the destroyer
of the garrisoned castles of your foes.
And you have forged for yourself
war anklets from the gold of their crowns.
You have risen to an exalted state
while your detractors
are steeped in shame.
Your admirers bask in glory.
Let me see you in this state
in future too,
always sweet in words
and easily accessible.

—Avur Mulankilar on Killivalan, the Chola king

PURANANURU 40

They dream of meteors

Even the god of death
bides his time;
but you annihilate
your enemies with powerful forces
the moment you wish their death.
Scared of your striking power
they have nightmares.
They dream of meteors falling in all directions,
of tall trees shedding their leaves
and dying instantly,
of the sun going up in flames,
of birds letting out heart-rending shrieks,
of teeth dropping to the ground,
of the body rubbed with oil,
of wild hogs mating,
of men losing their garments
and their weapons of war
collapsing to the ground.
They live in constant terror of you
in their unsafe homes
hiding their sorrow from their wives
by kissing their children's eyes.
Thus in great confusion
are the lands of your adversaries
for you have advanced on them
like raging fire and gusty winds.

—Kovur Kilar on Killivalavan, the Chola king

PURANANURU 41

One man fighting another

One man
fighting another,
killing him or getting killed
is nothing new
in this world.
But here is a warrior
the like of whom has never been heard of—
resplendent in his form,
wearing the dark, tender shoots of *vembu*
along with the flower stalks of *ulignai*,
and closely woven garlands of nectar-fresh flowers
and displaying ornaments of gold.
How handsome he is
with all the pride of a conqueror!
Singers sing his praises
with songs to the accompaniment
of the *kinai*'s beat.
Not knowing his greatness
seven of his enemies
joined together and said,
'We will fight him.'
And all the seven
single-handedly he fought
and killed in the field.

—Idaikundrur Kilar on Neduncheliyan, the Pandyan king

PURANANURU 76

After a cold dip at the city gates

After a cold dip at the city gates,
wearing a wreath of neem shoots,
Cheliyan of terrible wars,
treading like an elephant
has arrived at the battlefield,
the kinai drums heralding his approach.
His foes are many.
Perhaps some of them may yet survive.
For daytime is a little too short.

—Idaikundrur Kilar on Neduncheliyan, the Pandyan king

PURANANURU 79

Leaning on the pillar

Leaning on the pillar
of your little house
you ask me, girl,
the whereabouts of my son.
I am blest if I know that.
This womb that bore him
is like a den
abandoned by a tiger
after a brief stay.
Perhaps he will be found
in some battlefield.

—Kavarpendu

PURANANURU 86

Keep off, enemies!

Keep off, enemies,
from the battlefield!
For among us
is a veteran soldier,
strong as a chariot wheel
which a carpenter
with the skill to make
eight chariots a day
laboured for a month to shape.

—Avvaiyar on Athiyaman Neduman Anji

PURANANURU 87

Can any herd of deer . . .

Can any herd of deer,
in the foothills
where the *kanthal* blooms
resembling broken bangles
and wild jasmine unfolding
amidst lush green bushes
spread their combined fragrance,
stand before a charging tiger?
Can any patch of darkness cling
to the murky corners of the sky
when the dazzling sun comes out?
And when a lordly bull
pulling a heavily loaded carriage,
axle bending under the weight
and wheels sinking into the soil,
walks with vigorous strides
throwing up the sand
and trampling rocks to pieces,
is there any obstacle
which he cannot overcome?
In the same manner,
O warrior king,
with long ebony arms
reaching down to your thighs
and hands unfailing,
when you enter the battlefield,

is there any soldier on earth
to defeat you
and exult over the capture
of your vast country?

—Avvaiyar on Athiyaman Neduman Anji

PURANANURU 90

The lisp of children

The lisp of children
is no music.
It is often unintelligible
and inopportune.
Yet, to a father
it is so heartwarming.
Even so
are my words to you
Neduman Anji,
conqueror of many a garrisoned fort.
And you bestow your loving grace
on me.

—Avvaiyar on Athiyaman Neduman Anji

PURANANURU 92

Like a mighty elephant

Like a mighty elephant
lying docilely in the ford
letting village children
scrub his white tusks,
you are gentle to us, king.
And like the selfsame elephant
in his state of musth,
you are a terror to your foes.

—Avvaiyar on Athiyaman Neduman Anji

PURANANURU 94

Used and unused

Here,
your weapons
are decked with flowers
and peacock feathers.
Their strong rounded shafts
well oiled and polished,
they are kept in a guarded mansion.
But there,
the weapons of my patron—
who is the head of the brotherhood of the poor,
who gives away
while there is plenty
and shares what he has
when there is not much to give—
having ploughed into the hearts of foes
are broken and blunted.
They now lie
in the blacksmith's forge.

—Avvaiyar on Athiyaman Neduman Anji when Thondaiman
displayed his armoury

PURANANURU 95

Two enemies

The young son of my leader,
who has a broad, handsome chest
adorned with fresh-blown thumbai blooms
and long, sturdy arms
has two enemies.

One is women,
enamoured of him
their flower-like, black-dyed eyes
lose their brightness
and their arms wane thin.

And the other,
villagers of his enemy land
who, even on non-festive days
used to feast with their kin
on rice and mutton
now flee their homes,
afraid that his war elephants may come
marauding into the village
and drink from their springs.

—Avvaiyar on Poguttelini, son of Athiyaman

PURANANURU 96

As cordial as on the first day

I did not visit him
for a day or two.
I visited him
day after day
and took along with me
many other minstrels.
Yet he was as cordial
as he was on the first day.
Such a one is Athiyaman,
with his well-sculpted chariot
and decorated elephants.
Sometimes the gifts may be
delayed a little,
but you are sure to get them
as sure as the elephant gets without fail
the balls of food
put between his tusks.
Therefore, my yearning heart,
have no fears.
May his feet be praised!

—Avvaiyar on Athiyaman Neduman Anji

PURANANURU 101

Like a spare axle

The oxen are young
and not accustomed to the yoke.
The wagon carries a heavy load
and has to travel uphill and downhill.
Who knows what will happen on the road?
So, the salt traders have a spare axle
fixed to the wagon's underside.

You are like that spare axle, o prince.
You have a powerful protecting hand
enjoying much renown.

And you hold sway like the full moon.
Will there be any darkness, then,
to those who live under your care?

—Avvaiyar on Poguttelini, son of Athiyaman

PURANANURU 102

Like a crocodile in water

Take care, you soldiers,
listen to my words:

My chief is like a crocodile, which,
though lying in shallow knee-deep water
muddied by the playing of village children
still has the power
to attack an elephant bull
and bring him down.

If you slight him
thinking of him as but a young man
knowing nothing about his
many subtle acts of ingenuity,
you will never win.

—Avvaiyar on Athiyaman Neduman Anji

PURANANURU 104

Bounteous Pari

Though neither good nor bad
gods do not refuse
the modest milkweed flowers
blooming in clusters
among dull-coloured leaves.
In the same manner,
even if fools and weaklings
visit him,
bounteous Pari
heaps them with gifts.

—Kapilar on Pari

PURANANURU 106

There is also rain

Repeatedly gifted poets sing
of Pari, praising him alone.
But Pari is not the only one
who succours the world.
There is also rain.

—Kapilar on Pari

PURANANURU 107

He will give himself

The firewood
with which a hill woman
lit a fire
being sandalwood,
the pleasant smoke from it
wafts into the blossoming branches
of the *vengai* tree
on the neighbouring mountain slope.
Such is the Parambu hill,
given as a gift to the singers.
Even if the singers
come begging for his own person
Pari, righteous soul,
will not say 'no'.
He will give himself to them.

—Kapilar on Pari

PURANANURU 108

Not by force

Pitiable indeed is the plight
of this big, dark hill.
It is not easy for kings
to take it by force.
But the minstrel
can easily win it
if she comes singing
and playing her kinai drum.

—Kapilar on Pari

PURANANURU 111

When the moon was full

In such a night as this
when the moon was full
our father was with us
and our hill
was our own.
But tonight
the moon is full again,
the triumphant kings
marching with their battle drums
have our hill,
and we are fatherless.

—Pari Makalir, daughters of Pari

PURANANURU 112

149

More than the raindrops

It is easy for anyone
to give away chariots as gifts
in drunken stupor.
But much renowned Malaiyan
has given these chariots
in sobriety.
And their number is more
than the raindrops falling
on the Mullur hills.

—Kapilar on Malaiyaman Thirumudikkari

PURANANURU 123

Never says no

The poets who sing in praise
of Thirumudikkari,
who is the lord of the hills
where waterfalls make steady music,
will not return empty-handed
even if they
start out on unlucky days,
when birds of ill omen intrude,
approach him at the wrong moment
and speak without tact.

—Kapilar on Malaiyaman Thirumudikkari

PURANANURU 124

The cow elephants in his land

O Aai,
do the cow elephants in your land
give birth to ten calves at a time?

If one would count the elephants
you gave with a smiling face as gifts
to those who sang in praise of
you and your hills
they would far outnumber
the spears that were thrown
when you defeated
the Kongars of the western seas.

—Uraiyur Enicheri Mudamosiyar on Aai Andiran

PURANANURU 130

This magnificent forest

This magnificent forest
abounds with elephants!
Did the forest too sing the praise of the hills,
capped by rain-bearing clouds,
of Aai,
who wears laurel flowers
and wields a terrible sword?

—Uraiyur Enicheri Mudamosiyar on Aai Andiran

PURANANURU 131

No vendor of virtues

Aai
is no vendor of virtues
to seek gain in an afterlife
for acts performed in this.
His charity rests on his conviction
on the ideals
held high by the saintly.

—Uraiyur Enicheri Mudamosiyar on Aai Andiran

PURANANURU 134

Reckless in charity

Not only on dried-up lakes
and needy fields,
but on waste lands too
the showers fall . . .
drawing no line.
So does Pegan,
who wears war anklets
and rides an angry, musth-producing elephant.
He draws no line while giving.
Such a person is he,
reckless in charity
but never so in the battlefield.

—Paranar on Pegan

PURANANURU 142

Give them all

There are those who love you;
those whom you love.
And you have many kinsfolk, too,
who are hungry and in dire need.
There are also people
whom you owe.
Let them all be benefited, my dear.
You need have no thoughts of prudence
that we should be worldly-wise.
Distribute the riches among them all
without any discrimination—
the riches which Kumanan,
the ruler of the Mudirai hills
abounding in fruits,
has showered on us.

—Perunchithiranar on Kumanan

PURANANURU 163

The world keeps going

The world keeps going
because there live in it
men who will not eat alone
even ambrosia from the gods;
men who do not hate;
men who do not remain torpid
fearing things that others fear.
They'd lay down their lives
in deeds of fame,
but will not do any wrong
even if the whole world
is laid at their feet.
And they are tireless.
Having all these fine qualities,
they strive hard,
not for their own good
but for the good of others.

—Ilamperuvaluthi, the Pandyan king

PURANANURU 182

If an elephant is fed

If an elephant is fed
with rice
harvested from the fields,
even a small strip of land
will feed him for days.
But when the elephant
enters the fields to forage,
more rice is trampled upon
than eaten.
Acres of land lie ravaged.
Likewise, when a wise king
collects his taxes
methodically,
his coffers will be full
and the country too will prosper.
But when a weak king
and his ignorant, ostentatious officers
harass the people for taxes
his kingdom will be like the fields
trampled by the elephant.
He gets nothing
and his country, too, will suffer.

—Pisirandaiyar on Arivudainambi, the Pandyan king

PURANANURU 184

The driver and his carriage

When the driver of the carriage,
wheels and shaft fastened in place,
is efficient,
the carriage runs smoothly
and meets with no harm on the way.
But when the driver knows not how to drive,
the carriage gets bogged down
in a mire of difficulties
and meets with more and more ills
all along the way.

—Thondaiman Ilanthiraiyan

PURANANURU 185

Neither food grain nor water

Neither food grain
nor water
is life to the wide world.
The king himself
is its life.
Therefore, it is imperative
that the king
with his victorious army
keeps in mind
that he is life to his people.

—Mosi Keeranar

PURANANURU 186

As good as the men

Whether it is country
or jungle,
whether it is low-lying
or mountainous,
it does not matter.
You are as good
as the men who live on you,
O earth.
All hail to you!

—Avvaiyar

PURANANURU 187

A measure of grain

A sovereign king
holding unrivalled sway
over his sea-girt land,
and a savage
setting a snare for some wild animal
and watching over it night and day,
both have the same needs:
a measure of grain to eat
and a set of clothes to wear.
Other needs too
are the same.
So the use of wealth
is to give it away.
If you desire to have it
all to yourself,
take care,
there is many a slip.

—Nakkeeranar, son of Madurai Kanakkayan

PURANANURU 189

Rats and tigers

A rat in a rice field
waits till the crops are ripe
and then steals the grains
and stores them in his hole.
Some men are like these rats
hoarding wealth without shame.
Let us not have
the friendship of such men;
but let us befriend
men who are like tigers.
For a tiger hunting for food
is so proud
that he will not eat
if the boar he attacks
falls to his left.
He starves that day.
The next day he goes
with an angry roar,
attacks a young elephant bull
and fells him to his right.
Only then does he eat.
Let us have as friends
men of such dignity.

—Nalluruthiran, the Chola king

PURANANURU 190

Without worries

'How is it that
you have no grey hair
even at this ripe old age?'
you ask me.
Let me tell you:
My wife is a gem of a woman.
My sons and daughters
are full of virtue.
My household servants
are quick to read my mind.
My country is protected
by a king
who commits no wrong.
And my native village
is full of elder men
of profound learning,
wisdom and humility.

—Pisirandaiyar

PURANANURU 191

All the world is our home

All the world is our home.
All men our kin.
Good and evil
are not caused by others.
Nor are suffering and relief.
We do not exult
that life is sweet,
nor do we cry
in bitterness
that life is cruel.
We know from the vision of seers
that life takes its fated course
like a raft that floats
on a rapid river
roaring among the rocks
during the monsoon rains.
Therefore we neither marvel at the great
nor disdain the small.

—Kaniyan Punkundran

PURANANURU 192

The world is cruel

In one house
funeral drums
play their plaintive notes
while in another
sweet melodies
are overflowing.
Lovers united
wear ornaments of flowers
while parted lovers
shed tears of sorrow.
Thus are things ordained
by the One who has no attributes.
The world is cruel indeed.
Let those who know
the nature of life
find what is good.

—Pakkudukkai Nankaniyar

PURANANURU 194

Worthies, O worthies

Worthies, O worthies,
with wrinkled faces
hollow cheeks
and grey hair
like the rib bones of the *kayal* fish,
you have led so far
a wasted life.
You will rue this
when the One with his
deadly axe and cruel powers
approaches you.
So listen:
If you cannot do any good
refrain at least from doing evil.
Not only it pleases all,
but leads you on the right path.

—Nariveruuthalaiyar

PURANANURU 195

Give what you can

To give what you can
and refuse what you cannot
is a gesture of friendliness
that comes of the spirit of enterprise.
But to promise what you cannot give
and refuse what you can
is not only being hard on those
who ask you a favour,
it also brings down your reputation
as a patron.
However, I speak with no bitterness.
May you live long
and may your children prosper.
While I go away from here
braving the sun and the cold winds,
thinking of my delicate young wife
whose virtue is her loyalty
and who lives in my home
which is but a wind shelter
where my poverty
as if made of stone
is sitting tight.

—Avur Mulankilar on Nanmaran, the Pandyan king

PURANANURU 196

Ripe with fruit

When a magnificent banyan tree
is ripe with fruit,
clamouring birds visit it every day.
They don't tell themselves
'We had our fill yesterday,'
and stop coming.
So are the minstrels
visiting bounteous patrons.
The riches of the patrons
are theirs.
And so is their penury.

—Perumpathumanar

PURANANURU 199

It is disgraceful to beg

It is disgraceful to beg.
It is even more disgraceful
not to give.
It is ennobling to give.
But it is even more ennobling
not to accept.
Though the turbulent sea
is a vast expanse of clear water,
no one goes to it
to quench their thirst.
But a pool of drinking water,
though small
and made muddy
by sheep and cattle,
has many a track leading up to it.
So, the minstrels
who do not receive gifts sometimes
will not blame their patrons.
They'd rather blame it
on bird omens or on bad times.
And I am not angry with you
Ori, may you live long!
For you are as bounteous and limitless
as the monsoon clouds.

—Kalaithin Yanaiyar on Valvil Ori

PURANANURU 204

Many are the patrons

Arise, my heart,
let us go away from here.
There is no sign of love.
We are treated
as if we are strangers.
We don't want these gifts
that haven't come from the heart.
And to those who seek
recognition of merit,
with dignity,
the world is large
and many are the patrons
who really care.
Let us not lose heart,
but walk away with a lion's dignity.
Who would tarry here
hankering after unwilling gifts?

—Perunchithiran on Ilaveliman

PURANANURU 207

Crossing many a crag and hill

Crossing many a crag and hill
I came here,
of course, for gifts.
But how did he know me,
this warrior king,
to be so easy
with his gifts
without even seeing me?
I am no money grabber
to accept these riches
given with indifference.
I will accept with pleasure
however small a gift is,
if given with love
and after due recognition.

—Perunchithiranar on Athiyaman Neduman Anji

PURANANURU 208

Like minds come together

Even as gold, coral, pearls
and precious stones from the hills
though found in places far apart
are strung together
when a costly ornament is made,
noble minds mingle with noble minds
while the lowly men
seek their own kind.

—Kannaganar

PURANANURU 218

A monument of stone

He gave to the singers
and gained much fame.
He gave to the dancers
and won many a heart.
Men of virtue paid him homage.
His sceptre was never bent.
Men of wisdom paid him tributes.
His friendship was constant.
Gentle and sweet to women,
and tough against tough men,
he was a refuge
to the noble-minded.
But ignoring his greatness
thoughtless Death
has claimed this worthy soul.
Let us come together
in our sorrow,
O poets of truthful words,
and condemn Death
which,
plunging the world in sorrow
has made
our great patron
of unblemished glory
a monument of stone.

—Pothiyar on the death of Kopperuncholan

PURANANURU 221

174

Like a minstrel

Death wouldn't have claimed
the life of King Valavan,
who headed a winning army
and rode a sturdy chariot,
if it had confronted him
with an aggressive heart
or in an angry encounter.
Like a minstrel
it must have bowed before him
in obeisance,
sung his praise,
and begged him
to give up his life.

—Marokathu Nappasalaiyar on Killivalavan, the Chola king

PURANANURU 226

Unwise death

Truthful Elini—
famed for his fighting sword,
under whose reign
cattle grazed in the forest without fear,
tired wayfarers found rest houses on desert ways,
grain on the threshing floor was left unguarded
and invading enemies were repulsed—
has died in battle.

Unrighteous Death,
you've more to lose
than this hungry earth
which now grieves like a motherless infant
unable to feed its kinsfolk.
You have acted
like a ruined peasant
who eats the seed grain
unmindful of a bumper crop.
If only you had spared this one life
you would've gained many more lives
on the battlefield in which he fought.

—Arisil Kilar on Elini's death

PURANANURU 230

176

It's living that counts

He
took girls with bangled wrists
wore flowers from the sacred grove
smeared himself with cool sandalwood paste
routed his foes
heaped praise on his friends
never fawned on the strong
nor bullied the weak
never supplicated before others
nor refused to give alms
won much fame in royal assemblies
resisted oncoming armies
and watched their fleeing backs
sped off on swift horses
rode chariots on long streets
went in procession on huge elephants
gave bowls of mead generously
satisfied the hunger of bards
and eschewed ambiguous words.

Thus he did
all that needed doing.
Now that he is dead,

what does it matter
whether you
bury him
or burn him?

—Peraiyil Muruvalar on Nambi Neduncheliyan

PURANANURU 239

No use for jasmine

Young men of this land
wear their wreaths no more
and bangled maidens
have stopped plucking flowers.
The minstrels who used to
reach the flowers with their *yals*
do it no more.
And the singing girls too
have put aside their flowers.
Why then are you in bloom
O jasmine
in the land of Ollai
after its ruler, hardy Chattan,
deft wielder of the spear
and brave winner of many a battle
is dead and gone?

—Kudavayil Keerathanar on Perumchathan's death

PURANANURU 242

The good old days

To think of the past
gives much grief:

Holding by their arms
the girls,
who play with their clay dolls
and swim in the cool pond,
we hugged them as they hugged us
and danced as they danced.
With our gang of friends,
who harboured no secrets,
we perched on the low-hanging branches
of the marudam tree.
And as bystanders watched with stupefaction
we plunged into the deep pond with a splash
and emerged triumphantly
displaying handfuls of sand from the bottom.
Where are those good old days
of our innocent boyhood
to us who now have grown old,
cough as we mumble a few words
and stumble as we walk with a metal-knobbed stick?

—Thodithalai Viluthandinar

PURANANURU 243

Past and present

Look at the hermit there,
who after a freshening bath
in the mountain torrents
is now sitting before the sacred fire
tending it with firewood
furnished by a wild elephant
and drying his long matted hair.
He was the young man
who once caused
the ornaments of many maidens,
living in large houses beautiful as in a painting,
to come loose.

—Marpithiyar

PURANANURU 251

Once a wolf

Look at this ascetic—
who wears matted hair
which has acquired
the colour of *thillai* leaves
with frequent wash in the waterfalls—
picking the thick *thali* leaves.
Once he had been a hunter
of sweet young girls
from many a home
catching them in his net of words.

—Marpithiyar

PURANANURU 252

Both young and old

Both young and old
have left the field
but you lie here
and cannot be lifted,
your bosom
kissing the dust.
How am I to tell our folk
of your fate,
waving my hand
stripped of bangles?
If your mother knows your fate
what would become of her poor self
who had been praising you
without cease
and telling everyone
that your wealth and prosperity
would be hers
like the ripe berries
of this village banyan tree
shared by noisy birds?

—Kayamanar

PURANANURU 254

I am afraid to shout

I am afraid to shout for help
in this tiger-infested place.
If I try to lift you by myself—
I can't hold your broad chest in my arms.
O may unrighteous Death
who has approached you cruelly
feel embarrassed like me.
Dear one, just hold my wrist
and try to walk a little,
we shall try at least to reach
the shade of the hill beyond.

—Vanparanar

PURANANURU 255

Make it larger!

Hear me, potter:
Like a little lizard
that travels with a cart,
perching on the wheel,
I had travelled all the way with him
crossing many a wilderness.
Have pity on me,
and make his funeral urn
a little oversize.

—Anon.

PURANANURU 256

Like the downy feathers

Like the downy feathers
of a fish-eating egret
she had white hair—
the old dame.
And when she heard the news
that her young son
fell in the battlefield
after displaying great courage
facing a war elephant
and killing him,
the overwhelming joy she felt
was far greater than the joy
she had when she gave birth to him.
And the tears she shed
were far more in number
than the raindrops
that fell among the bamboos
of the Vethirai hills.

—Punkan Uthiraiyar

PURANANURU 277

He strikes terror

It may be easy for others too
to defeat their enemies
blunting their weapons in the process.

But it is my lord
who strikes terror
into the hearts of his enemies
who flee from the very sight
of his army camp
like people fleeing from
a cobra's nest
or from the village square
where a killer bull roams
telling themselves,
'Our formidable foe is there.'
Only my lord,
raising his spear in triumph
has that reputation.

—Madurai Ilankanni Kosikanar

PURANANURU 309

A mother speaks

It is my duty
to give him birth
and bring him up.
It is the duty of his father
to make him a good warrior.
It is the duty of the blacksmith
to forge him a spear.
It is the duty of the king
to give him a good standing.
And it's the duty of the young man
to enter the battlefield,
sword in hand,
rout the enemy in battle
killing his elephants,
and come back victorious.

—Ponmudiyar

PURANANURU 312

Like a fire drill

He is capable
of revelling in his riches.
He gives away freely
to those who serve him
and to those who beg of him.
He is a boon companion
even to his enemies.
This is Neduman Anji.
He could, if he chose,
be quiet and unobtrusive
like a fire drill
kept in the eaves.
But when occasion demands
he is quick to explode
like the selfsame fire drill
sending out sparks of fire.

—Avvaiyar on Athiyaman Neduman Anji

PURANANURU 315

The spear with a difference

How unlike the spears of others
is that of the warrior of our village!

At times
it lies on the loft of his little house
gathering dust.

Sometimes
it is bathed in the pond,
decked with flowers
and taken out in procession
by virtuous women,
followed by the music of harps and songs,
and arrives at the battlefield
striking terror all over the world.
And there
it strikes at the royal elephant
of the enemy king with his ocean-like army.

—Viriyur Nakkanar

PURANANURU 332

With lily-like eyes

The paddy harvesters beat their drums.
The bees that had their hives
on the stalks of the bamboos
fly away scared.
The potters come and take the honey.
And in the bards' quarters,
they catch tiny fish and slice them for food.
Such is honest Thalumban's Oonur—
and this girl with lily-like eyes
reminds one of that lovely village.
If only her mother had not given birth to her,
the trees beside the ford
wouldn't have suffered
having elephants tethered to their trunks
and chariots parked in their shade.

—Paranar

PURANANURU 348

191

Fire in the tree

Wiping the sweat from his forehead
with the tip of his spear,
the king utters harsh words.
The girl's father, too
doesn't speak modestly
but walks tall.
If this be the stand they take,
then, alas, the girl
is sure to bring ruin
to her native city
just like the fire
that brings ruin to the tree
it is born in.

—Madurai Marutanilanakanar

PURANANURU 349

The burning ground

It lies across a tract
of barren land
dotted with straggling spurge.
Owls hoot there
in broad daylight.
And in the light of the funeral lamp
are seen she-ghouls
with wide open mouths.
And filled with clouds of smoke
this burning ground evokes fear.

Tears shed by loved ones
quench the white ashes of their lovers
that lie among the bones.
Thus the burning ground
has seen the back of everyone—
being the last refuge of all mankind.
But no one has seen it turn its back.

—Thayankannanar

PURANANURU 356

Not worth a single seed of mustard

This bountiful earth revolving
around the sun
is so impermanent
that seven men rise and fall
in a single day.
If you weigh
worldly life
against the life of the spirit,
it is not worth a single seed of mustard.
Therefore men of love
have renounced the world
and are the richer for it.
Those who have not
are the losers.

—Vanmikiyar

PURANANURU 358

Notes

Introduction

1. Kailasapathy, *Tamil Heroic Poetry*, p. 27.

2. *Kurunthokai* actually consists of 401 poems, and one poem has nine lines which transgresses the four to eight line limit. It has been suggested that this poem (234) could be the missing poem from *Nattrinai*. It is not the practice to count the invocatory song at the beginning.

3. *Tamil Lexicon*, Vol. 1, pp. 7–11 and Vol. 5, pp. 2803–12.

4. Kesavan Veluthat, 'Into the "Medieval" and Out of it: Early South India in Transition,' p. 8.

5. Kailasapathy, *Tamil Heroic Poetry*, p. 13.

6. Hart, *Poems of Ancient Tamil*, p. ix.

7. Manickam, *Tamil Kadhal*, pp. 14–16.

8. Ibid., p. 502.

9. Ibid., p. 326.

10. Kailasapathy, *Tamil Heroic Poetry*, p. 170.

11. Hart, *Poems of Ancient Tamil*, pp. 153–54.

12. Kailasapathy, *Tamil Heroic Poetry*, p. 152.

13. The dates in parentheses are indicative. I have generally followed the dates given in Arunachalam, *Tamil Ilakkiya Varalaru*.

14. Manickam, *Tamil Kadhal*, pp. 122–23.

15. Swaminatha Iyer, *En Charithiram* (Chennai: U.V. Swaminatha Iyer Library, 1997), p. 534.

16. A.K. Ramanujan's translations from Kannada have come in for sustained analysis. See Tejaswini Niranjana's *Siting Translation:*

History, Post-Structuralism, and the Colonial Context (Berkeley: University of California, 1992) for a critique; and for a rebuttal Vinay Dharwadker, 'A.K. Ramanujan's Theory and Practice of Translation,' in *Post-Colonial Translation: Theory and Practice*, eds. Susan Bassnett and Harish Trivedi (London: Routledge, 1999). His translations from Tamil await such close analysis and discussion.

Akam

KURUNTHOKAI

Page 3.
This poem is the basis for an elaborate mythology. According to Saiva tradition the author of the poem, Iraiyanar, is lord Siva himself. Towards helping a poor poet Dharumi to win a prize for clarifying the Pandyan king Neduncheliyan's doubt whether women's hair was naturally fragrant, Siva is said to have composed this poem. The divine answer was in the affirmative.

Page 5.
his son's mother: Refers to the concubine's refusal to acknowledge her as his wife.

'the *valai* fish . . . snatches away a ripe mango': an instance of an implicit metaphor; the suggestion is the hero's easy access to sexual pleasure.

'Adi pavai' has been the subject of scholarly disagreement. While it is customary to translate it as 'like a mirror image' it has also been argued that it refers to puppetry. Here therefore is another version:

This man—
from the village
where the *valai* fish in the wet field
snatches away
a ripe mango falling
beside the field—
has gone back to his son's mother
throwing to the wind
all his promises to me.
He now kow-tows
before that woman
and acts like her mirror image
lifting his hands and legs
as she does.

Page 6.
The lover threatens to shame himself in public by wearing a wreath of milkweed buds (not usually worn) and riding a dummy horse made of palm frond. It's a threat never carried out. This theme, in later centuries, evolves as a separate genre called Madal.

Page 9.
pallor of lovesickness: Lovesickness is said to cause paleness and discolouration of the girl's skin. A recurrent motif or trope in Tamil literature.

Page 14.
the darling of your heart: Rather than call herself only his wife, she claims she's 'the darling of your heart' to run down the concubine.

Page 19.
The water falls from a high place, similarly the young man falls from grace due to his blind love.

Page 20.
The hillman harvests a second crop of country beans after reaping the millet. The lover too is entitled to return to her after the first act of lovemaking.

Page 25.
bangles of a smaller size: A pining girl's wrist and arms are said to grow thin thus causing the bangles to slip off. Again a recurrent motif providing endless ways for the poets to improvise.

Page 43.
Pooli land: One of the twelve regions of the Tamil country where a corrupt form of Tamil is said to have been spoken.

Page 55.
like the nerunji flowers: The nerunji flower always turns towards the sun.

Page 56.
The suggestion is that rumour and gossip spread like the foul smell of drying fish.

Page 58.
plaintive note: The tune of vilari.

AINKURUNURU

Page 68.
your call of good omen: A common belief, persistent to this day, that the call of the crow augurs the arrival of a guest.

KALITHOKAI

Page 101.
yal: A stringed musical instrument like the harp.

Puram

PURANANURU

Page 122.
donkey ploughs: An ancient manner of humiliating defeated enemies. Enemy lands were ploughed with donkeys and sown with crabgrass and castor seeds to make them unfit for agriculture.

Page 123.
mulavu: A kind of drum.

Page 124.
except pregnant women: Pregnant women, during morning sickness, are said to eat soil.

Page 128.
kalangu: A women's game played with pebbles and pebble-like nuts.

Page 132.
Neduncheliyan, the Pandyan king, defeated seven foes including the Chera and Chola kings and five chieftains.

Page 133.
for daytime is a little too short: It was an ethic of war not to fight after dusk.

Page 140.
Composed when Athiyaman Neduman Anji was at war with Thondaiman and Avvaiyar went as an emissary to broker peace.

Page 149.
Composed by the daughters of Pari after the three crowned kings—Cheran, Cholan and Pandyan—laid siege on Pari's Parambu hill country and killed him by subterfuge.

Pages 152–53.
The chieftain Aai Andiran was known for his generosity with elephants.

Page 173.
Pisirandaiyar, the poet, was a friend of the Chola king Kopperuncholan though they never met each other. When the king died Pisirandaiyar too died by fasting facing the north. This poem was written on that occasion by Kannaganar.

Pages 191–92.
These two poems speak of the devastation visited upon a proud chieftain's clan for refusing to give the daughter in marriage to a king.

Select Bibliography

M.L. Thangappa in his typical style has used any edition that came to his hand to translate and, I suspect, often relied on memory as well. I have used the versions in the S. Rajam editions, the so-called Murray editions, published between 1957 and 1959, as the standard for text, stanza numbers, author, *thinai*, etc. Additionally, the editions of U.V. Swaminatha Iyer, the Saiva Siddhanta Mahasamajam (ed. S. Vaiyapuri Pillai), the Saiva Siddhanta Nurpathippu Kazhagam (especially the *Purananuru* commentary of Avvai S. Duraisamy Pillai) and the Tamil University (M. Shanmugam Pillai's *Kurunthokai*) have been consulted.

Arunachalam, Mu. *Tamil Ilakkiya Varalaru (Noottrandu Murai)*, 14 volumes. (Chennai: The Parkar, 2005, reprint).

Hart, George L. *The Poems of Ancient Tamil: Their Milieu and Their Sanskrit Counterparts*. (New Delhi: Oxford University Press, 1999).

Kailasapathy, K. *Tamil Heroic Poetry*. (Oxford: Clarendon Press, 1968).

Kulandai, Pulavar. *Tholkappiyar Kala Tamilar*. (Chennai: Pari Nilaiyam, 1959).

Mahadevan, Iravatham. *Early Tamil Epigraphy*. (Chennai and Cambridge [Mass.]: Cre-A and Harvard University Press, 2003).

Manickam, V.Sp. *Tamil Kadhal*. (Chennai: Pari Nilaiyam, 1962, reprint 1980). [Editor's note: Based on his PhD dissertation published as *The Tamil Concept of Love*, this Tamil version is vastly superior in nuance, argument, elaboration and style.]

Mehrotra, Arvind Krishna. *The Absent Traveller: Prakrit Love Poetry from the Gathasaptasati of Satavahana Hala*. (New Delhi: Ravi Dayal, 1991).

Sanjeevi, N. *Sanga Ilakkiya Attavanaikal*. (Chennai: University of Madras, 1973).

Selvamony, Nirmal. *Tolkaappiyam: Akattinaiiyal*. (Nagercoil: Sobitham, 1989).

Sivathamby, K. *Studies in Ancient Tamil Society*. (Madras: New Century Book House, 1998).

Tamil Lexicon, 7 volumes. (Chennai: University of Madras, 1982, reprint).

Thangappa, M.L. 'On Translating Sangam Poetry'. Unpublished ms.

_____. 'Mozhipeyarppil En Pattarivu'. In *On Translation*, ed. M. Valarmathi. (Chennai: International Institute of Tamil Studies, 1999).

Trautmann, Thomas. *Languages and Nations: The Dravidian Proof in Colonial Madras*. (New Delhi: Yoda, 2006).

Vaiyapuri Pillai, S. *Ilakkiya Chinthanaikal*. (Chennai: Vaiyapuri Pillai Ninaivu Mandram, 1989).

Veluthat, Kesavan. 'Into the "Medieval" and Out of it: Early South India in Transition'. Presidential address, Medieval Indian History Section, Indian History Congress, XLVIII Session, Bangalore, 1997.

Venkatachalapathy, A.R. 'A.K. Ramanujan: A Tribute'. *Economic and Political Weekly*, 31 July 1993.

_____. 'Poet-Translator as Essayist'. Review of *The Collected Essays of A.K. Ramanujan*. In *The Indian Review of Books*, April–May 2000.

_____. 'The Making of a Canon'. In *In Those Days There Was No Coffee: Writings in Cultural History*. (New Delhi: Yoda, 2006).